FAR OUT
FAIRY TALES

STONE ARCH BOOKS
a capstone imprint

INTRODUCING...

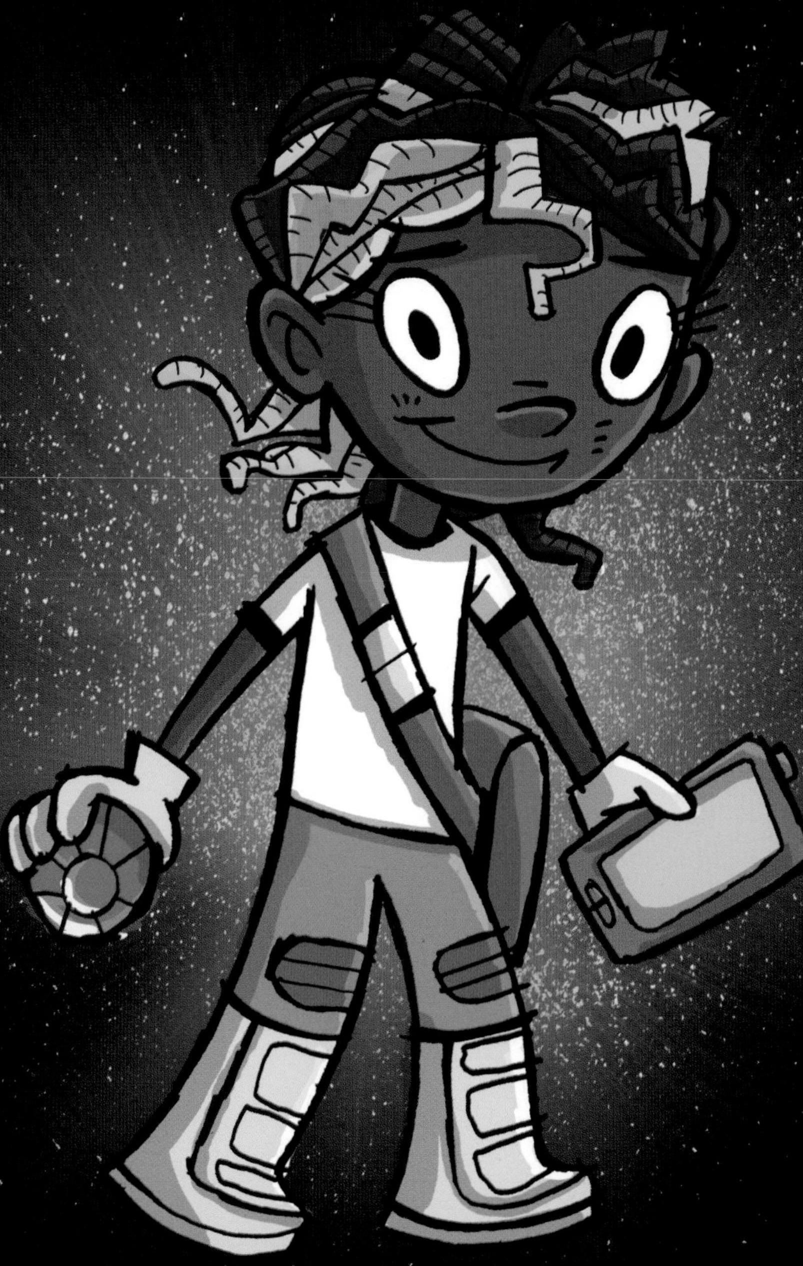

GOLDILOCKS

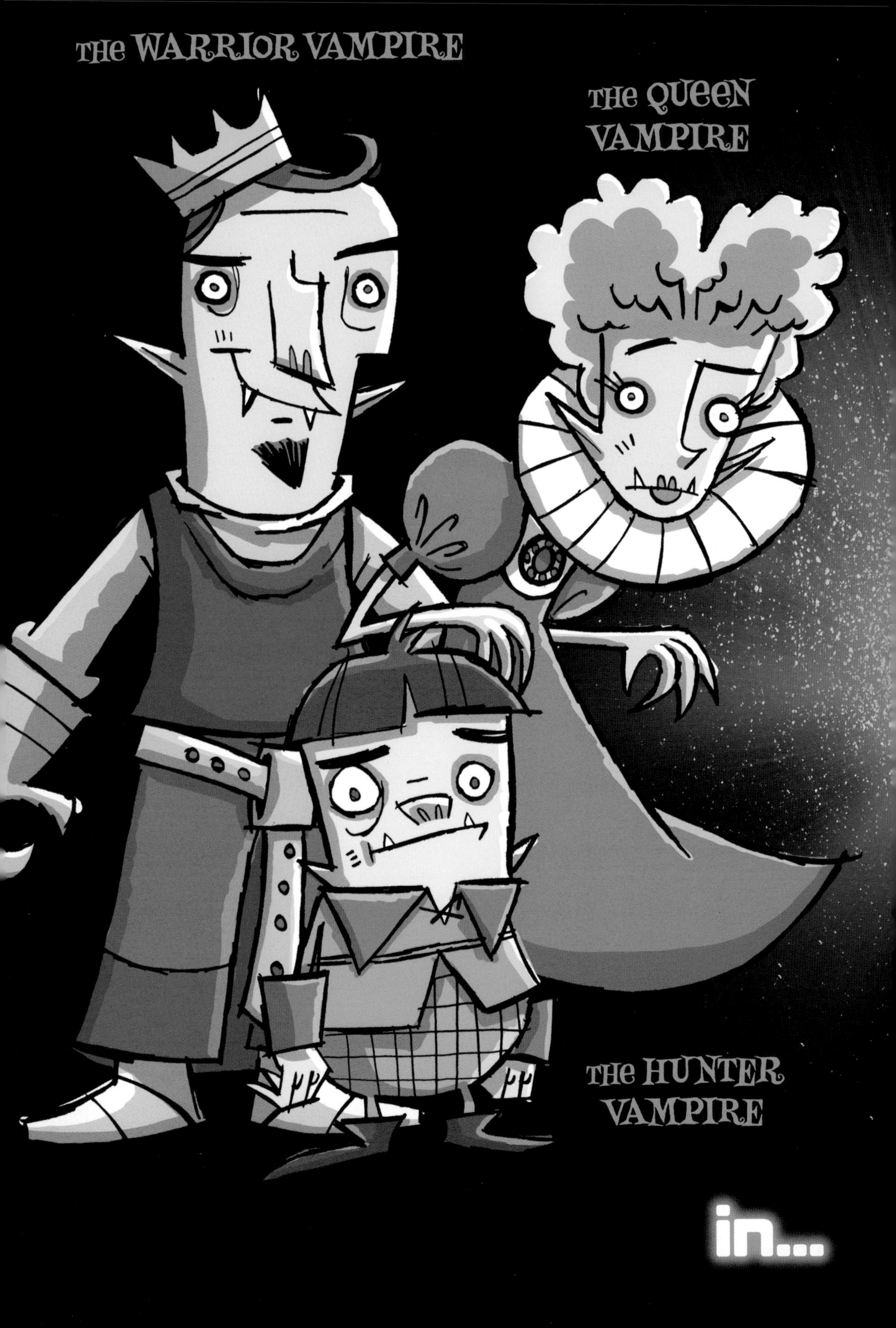
THE WARRIOR VAMPIRE
THE QUEEN VAMPIRE
THE HUNTER VAMPIRE
in...

Far Out Fairy Tales is published by
Stone Arch Books
A Capstone Imprint
1710 Roe Crest Drive
North Mankato, Minnesota 56003
www.mycapstone.com

Cataloging-in-Publication Data is
available at the Library of Congress
website.
ISBN 978-1-4965-3783-6 (hardcover)
ISBN 978-1-4965-3785-0 (paperback)
ISBN 978-1-4965-3787-4 (eBook PDF)

Summary: Goldilocks is an adventurer
extraordinaire. When her travels bring
her to a creepy crypt, she discovers
more than just dusty relics . . .
She's stumbled into the home of one,
two, THREE blood-sucking vampires!
Can Goldi use her smarts to defeat
the vampire trio, or is this her last
archaeological adventure?

Designed by Hilary Wacholz
Edited by Abby Huff
Lettering by Jaymes Reed

Printed and bound in the USA.
012018   011018R

FAR OUT FAIRY TALES

GOLDILOCKS

AND THE THREE

VAMPIRES

A GRAPHIC NOVEL

BY LAURIE S. SUTTON

ILLUSTRATED BY C.S. JENNINGS

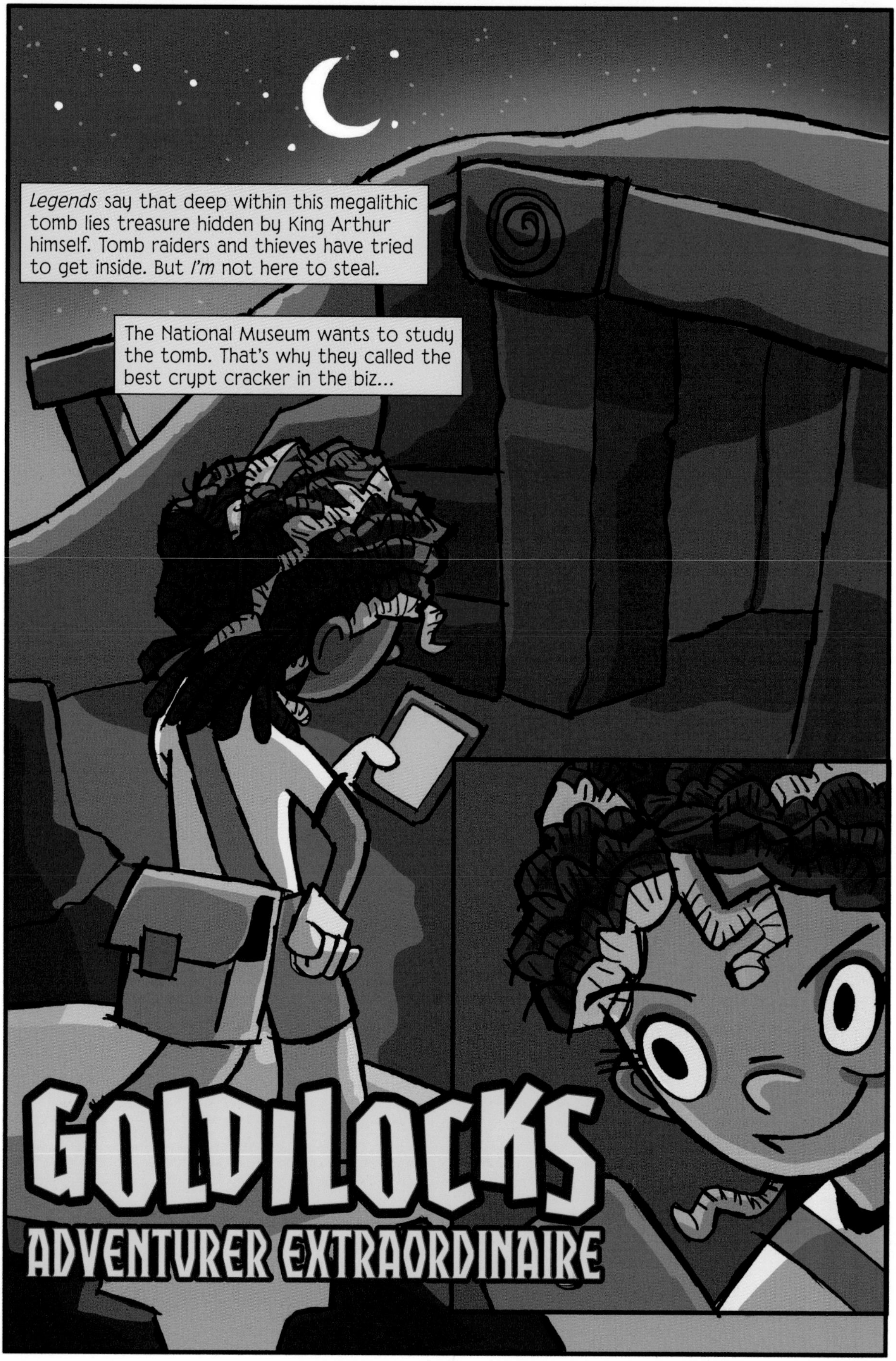
Legends say that deep within this megalithic tomb lies treasure hidden by King Arthur himself. Tomb raiders and thieves have tried to get inside. But *I'm* not here to steal.
The National Museum wants to study the tomb. That's why they called the best crypt cracker in the biz...
GOLDILOCKS
ADVENTURER EXTRAORDINAIRE

I've researched the tomb for months. Now I'm here right as the crescent moon is passing through the Ursa Major constellation--the Big Bear.

This *has* to be the key to opening the crypt.

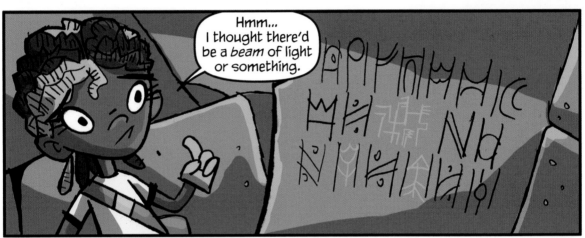

Hmm... I thought there'd be a *beam* of light or something.

There must be mica crystals in these symbols...They're reflecting light because of the angle of the rising sun at this exact time. I was right!

Thanks, dusty journals!

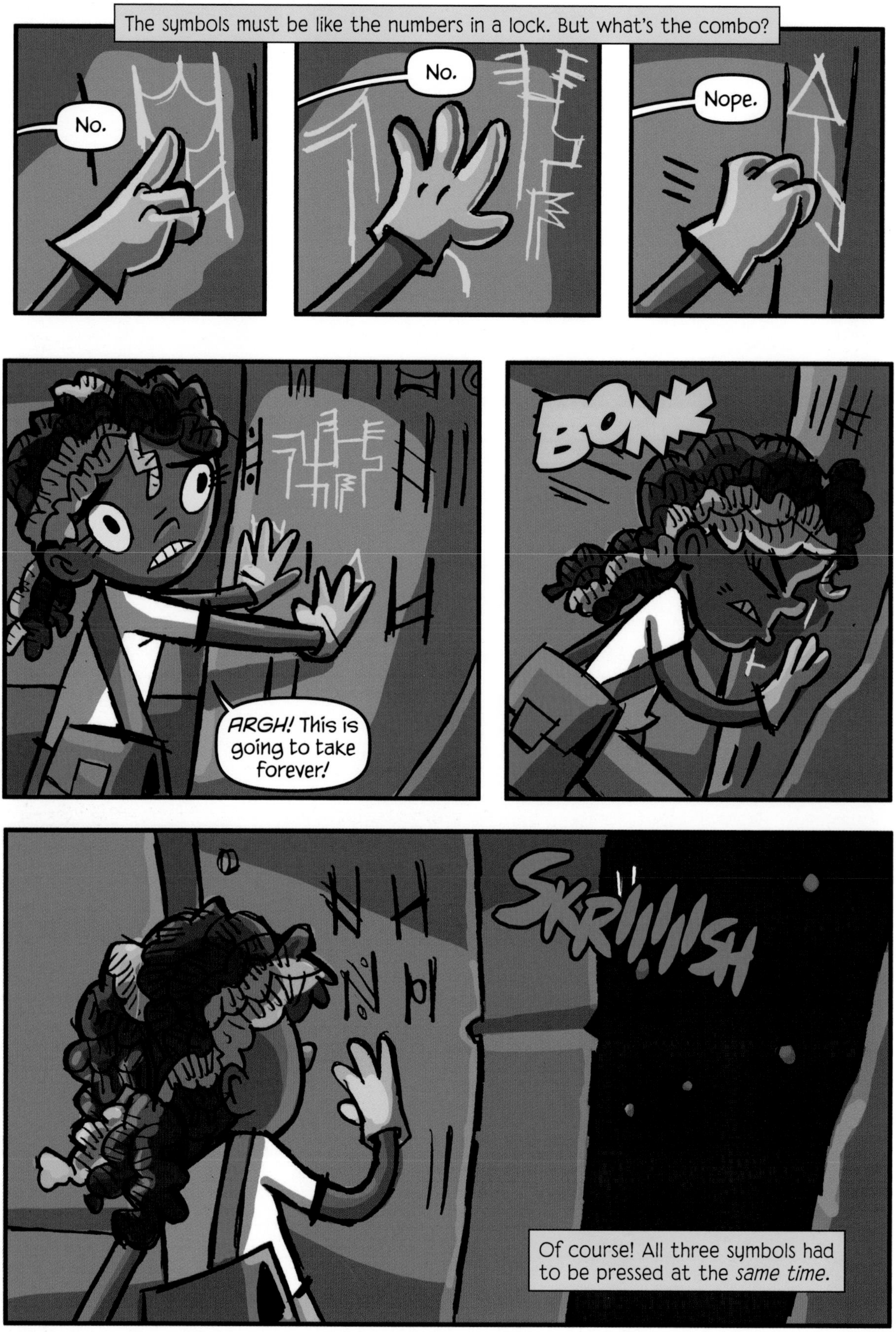

The symbols must be like the numbers in a lock. But what's the combo?
No.
No.
Nope.
ARGH! This is going to take forever!
BONK
SKRIIIIISH
Of course! All three symbols had to be pressed at the same time.

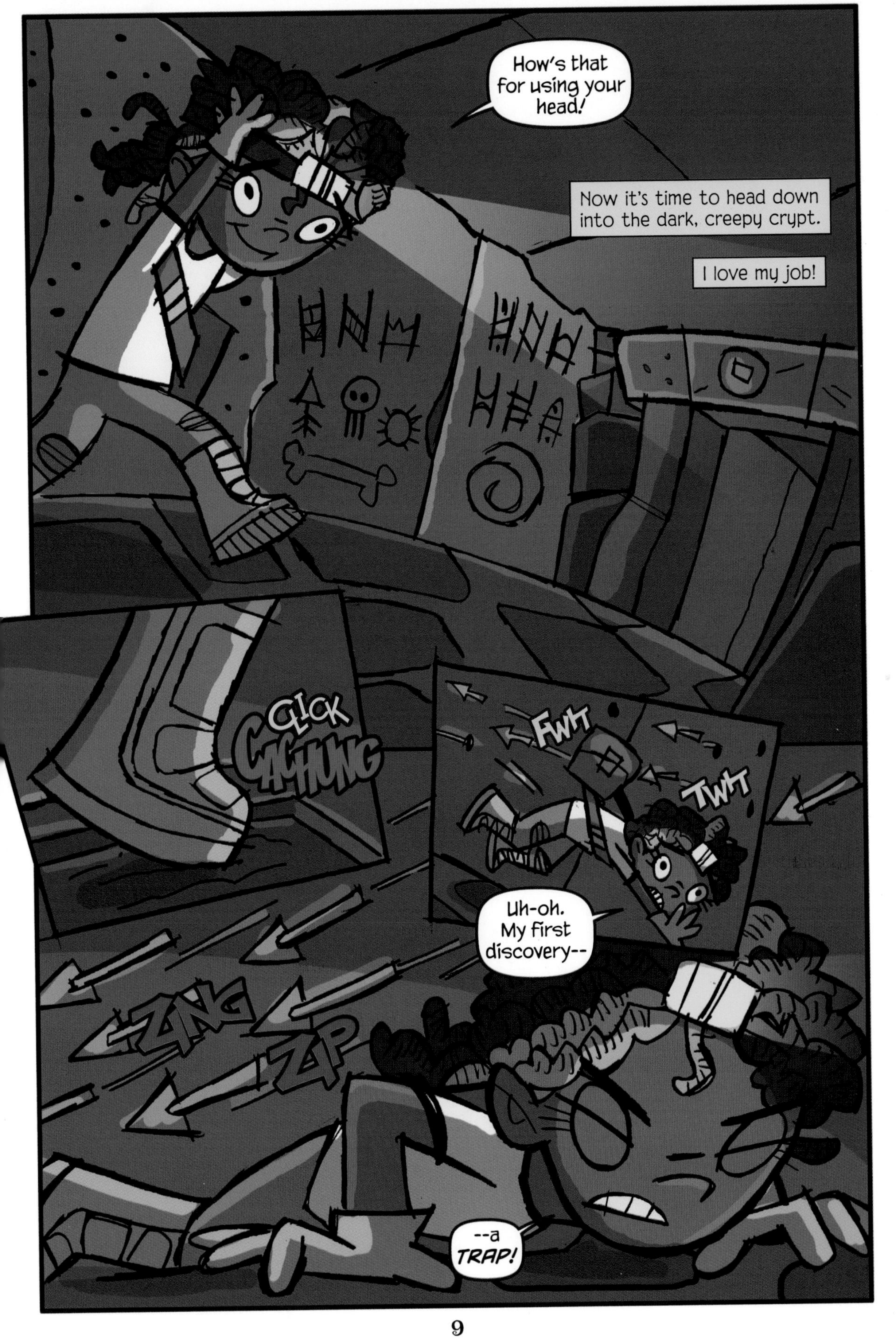
How's that for using your head!
Now it's time to head down into the dark, creepy crypt.
I love my job!
CLICK
CACHUNG
FWIT
TWIT
Uh-oh. My first discovery--
ZING
ZAP
--a TRAP!

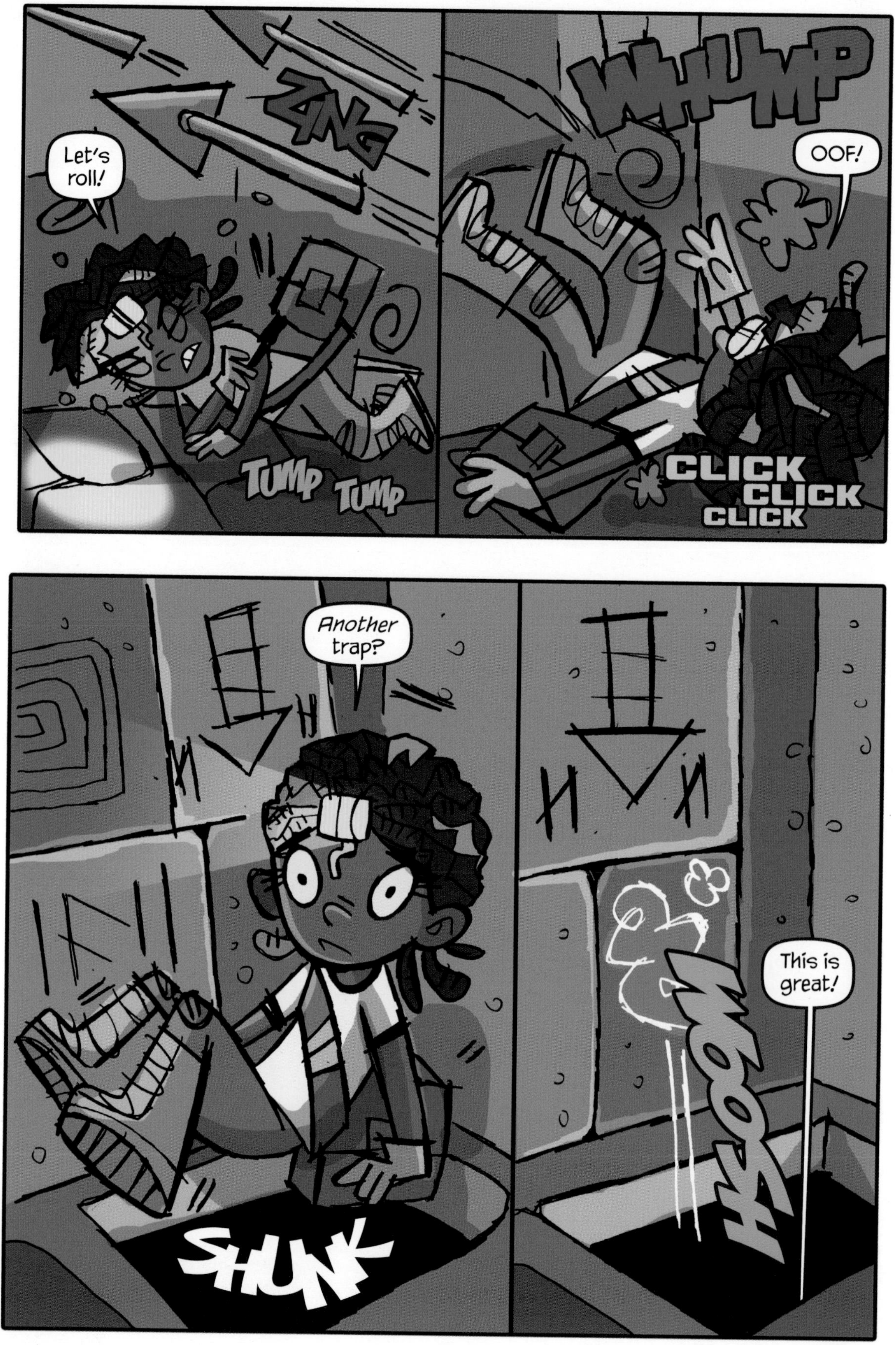
ZING
Let's roll!
TUMP TUMP
WHUMP
OOF!
CLICK CLICK CLICK
Another trap?
SHUNK
This is great!
WOOSH

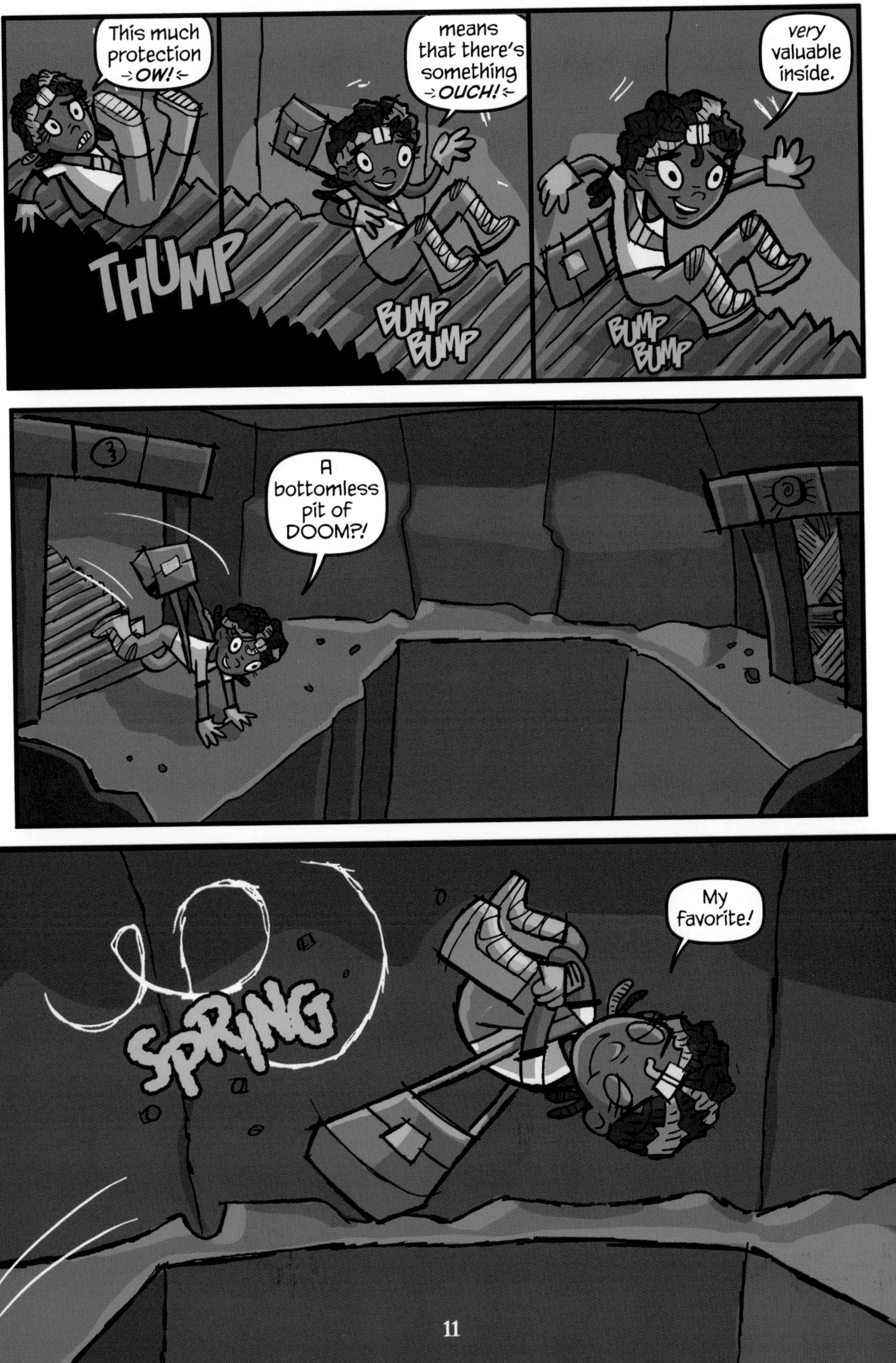
This much protection
OW!
THUMP
means that there's something
OUCH!
BUMP BUMP
very valuable inside.
BUMP BUMP
A bottomless pit of DOOM?!
SPRING
My favorite!

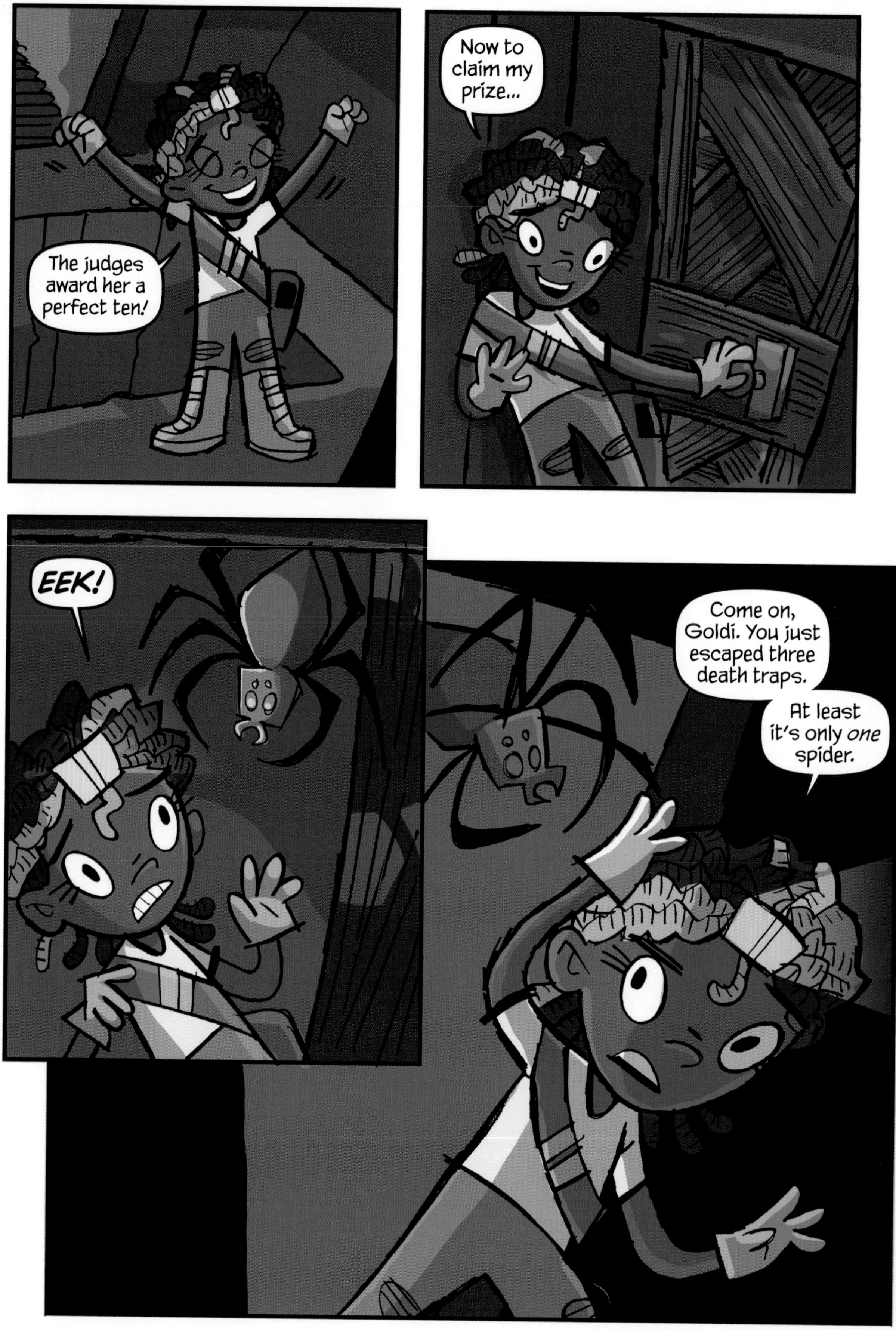
The judges award her a perfect ten!
Now to claim my prize...
EEK!
Come on, Goldi. You just escaped three death traps.
At least it's only *one* spider.

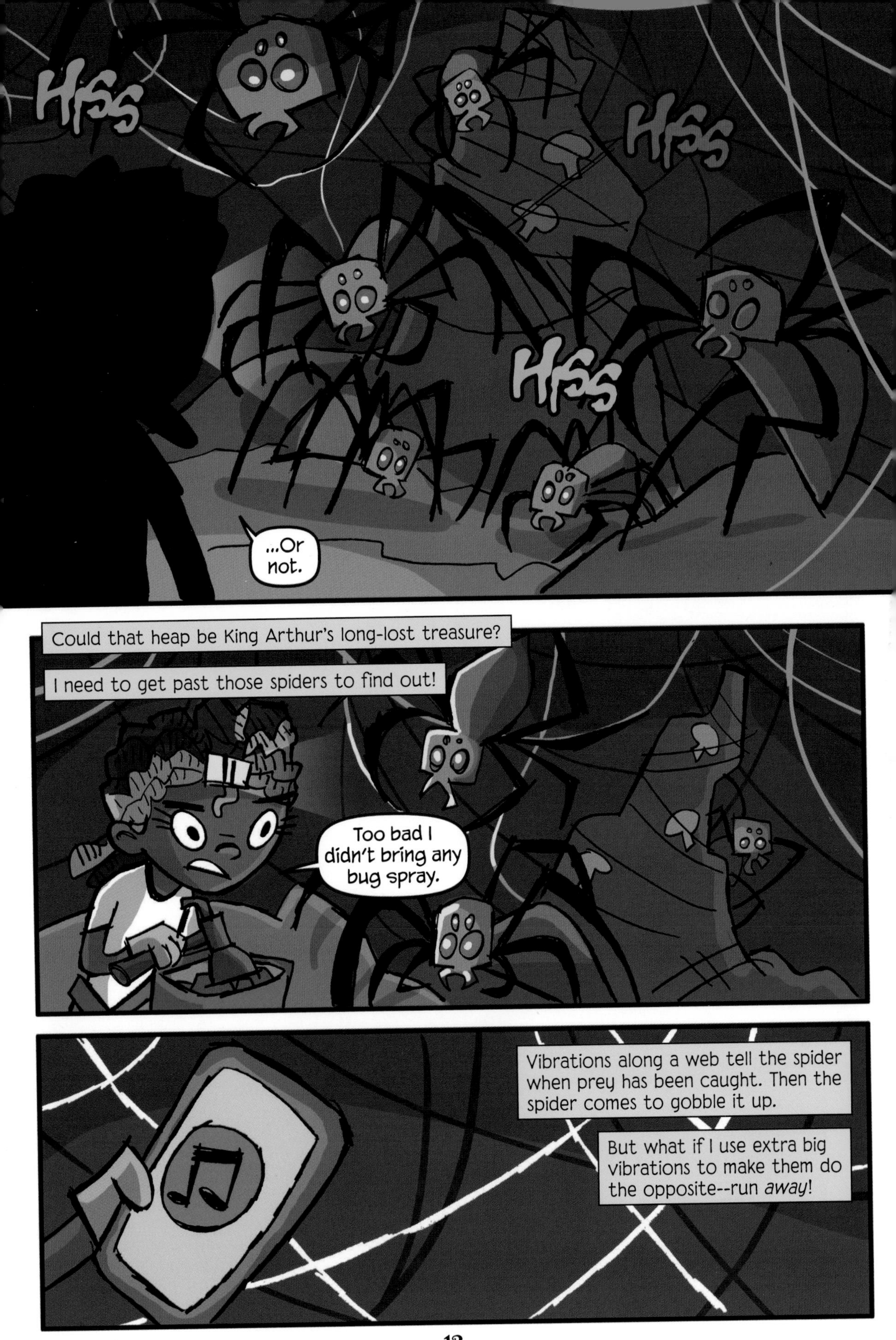

Hiss
Hiss
Hiss
...Or not.
Could that heap be King Arthur's long-lost treasure?
I need to get past those spiders to find out!
Too bad I didn't bring any bug spray.
Vibrations along a web tell the spider when prey has been caught. Then the spider comes to gobble it up.
But what if I use extra big vibrations to make them do the opposite--run *away*!

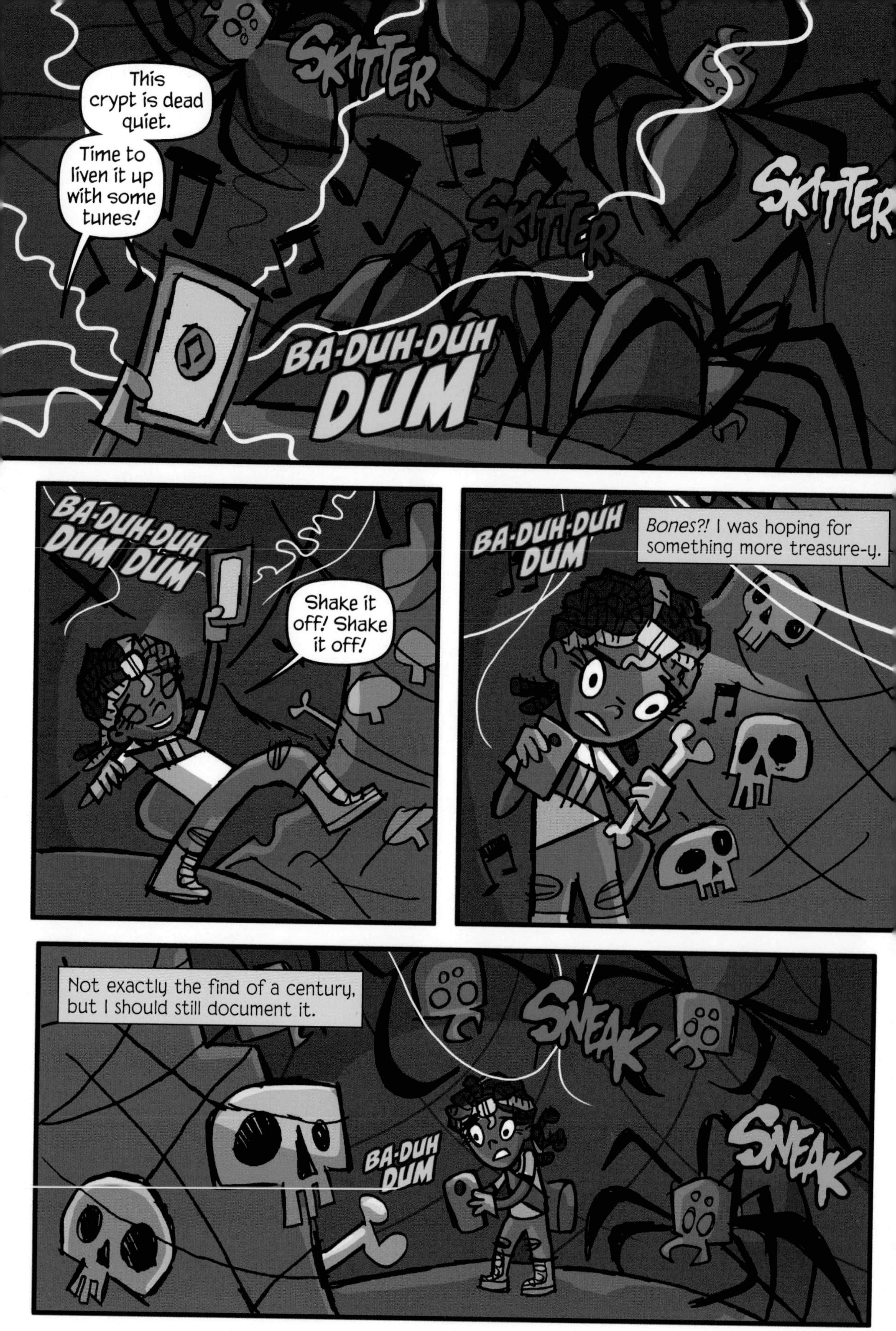
SKITTER
This crypt is dead quiet.
Time to liven it up with some tunes!
SKITTER
SKITTER
BA-DUH-DUH DUM
BA-DUH-DUH DUM DUM
Shake it off! Shake it off!
BA-DUH-DUH DUM
Bones?! I was hoping for something more treasure-y.
Not exactly the find of a century, but I should still document it.
SNEAK
BA-DUH DUM
SNEAK

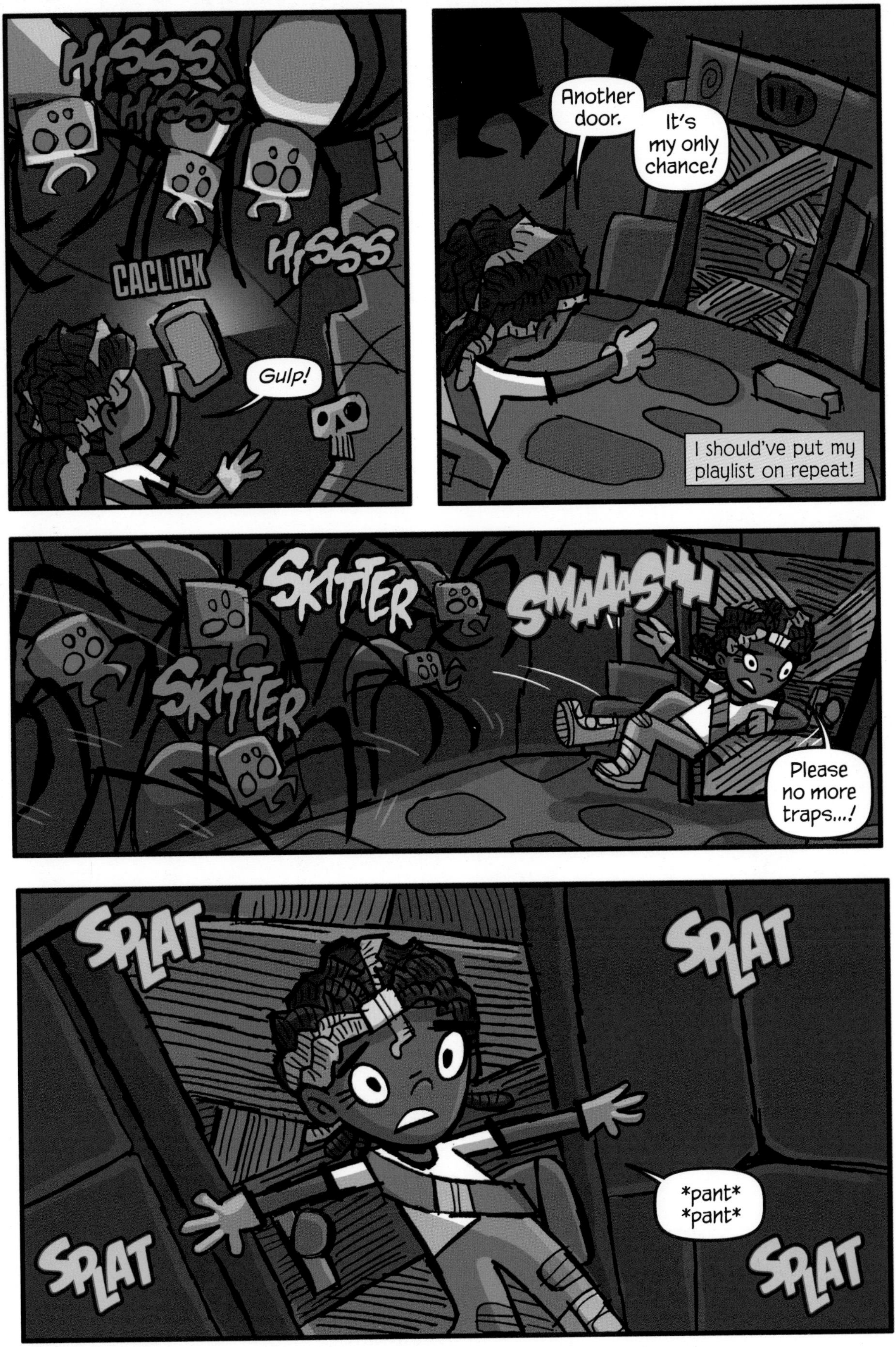
HISSS
HISSS
HISSS
CACLICK
Gulp!
Another door.
It's my only chance!
I should've put my playlist on repeat!
SKITTER
SKITTER
SMAAASHH
Please no more traps...!
SPLAT
SPLAT
SPLAT
SPLAT
pant *pant*

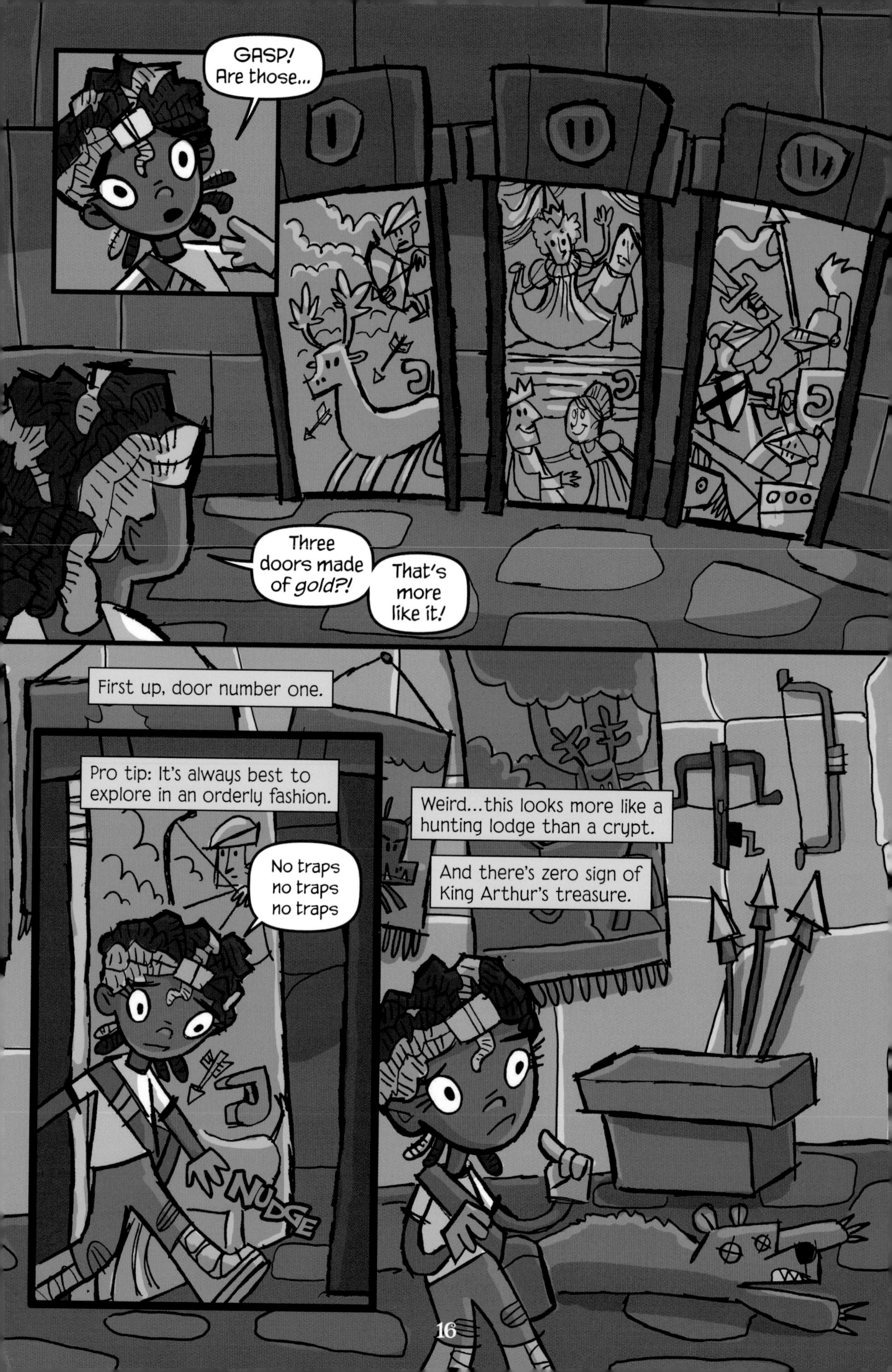
GASP! Are those...
Three doors made of *gold?!*
That's more like it!
First up, door number one.
Pro tip: It's always best to explore in an orderly fashion.
No traps no traps no traps
NUDGE
Weird...this looks more like a hunting lodge than a crypt.
And there's zero sign of King Arthur's treasure.

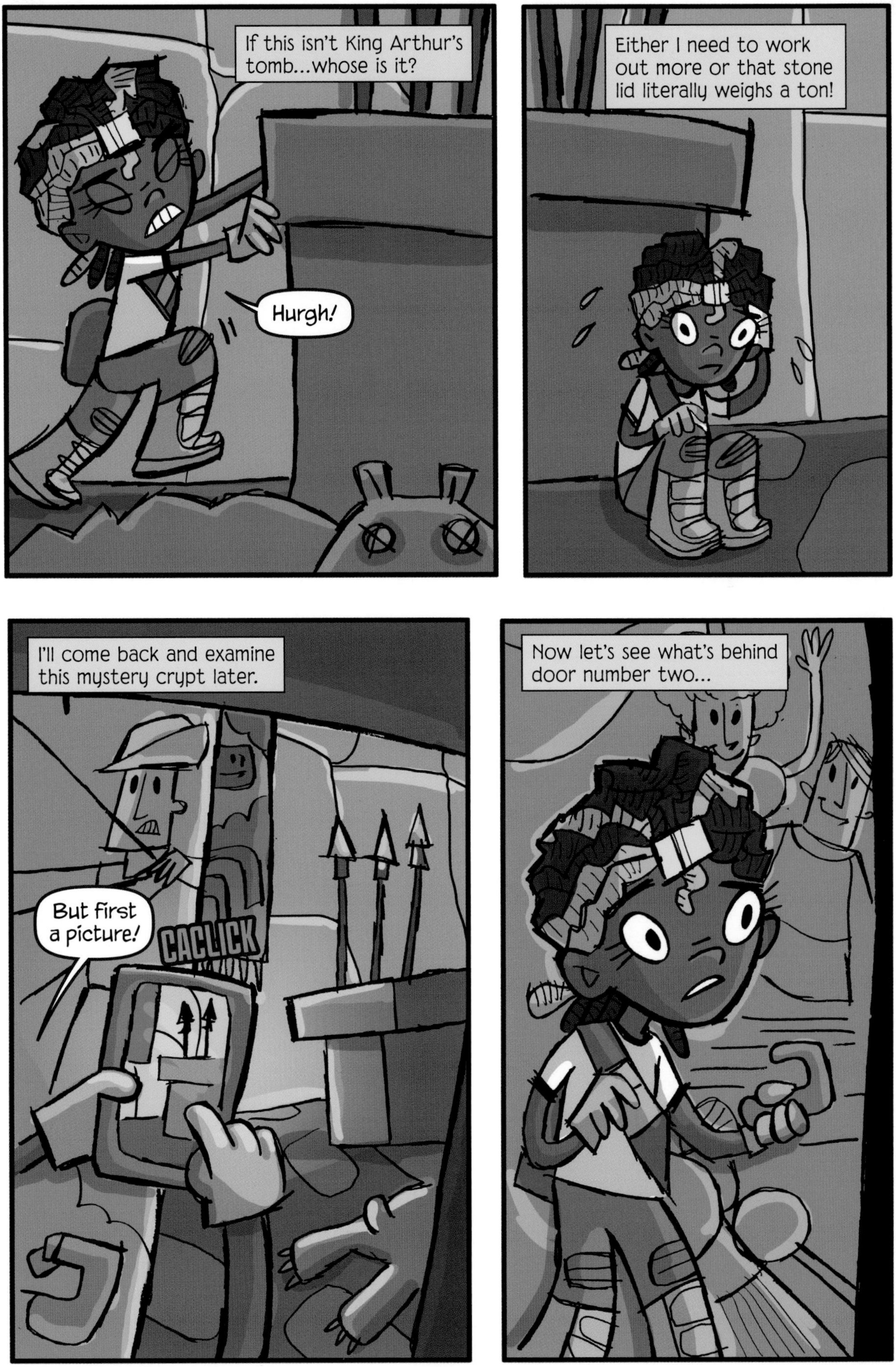

If this isn't King Arthur's tomb...whose is it?
Hurgh!
Either I need to work out more or that stone lid literally weighs a ton!
I'll come back and examine this mystery crypt later.
But first a picture!
CACLICK
Now let's see what's behind door number two...

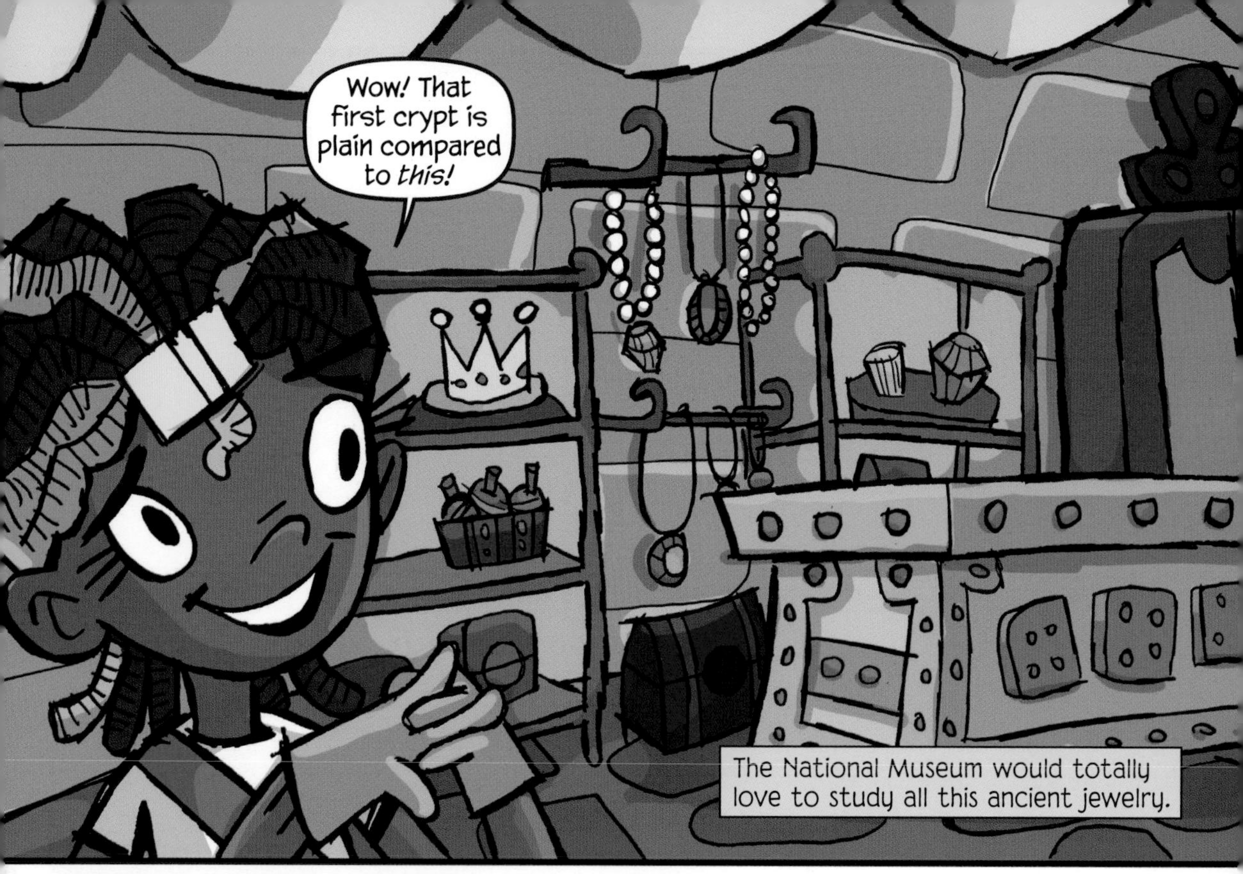
Wow! That first crypt is plain compared to *this!*
The National Museum would totally love to study all this ancient jewelry.

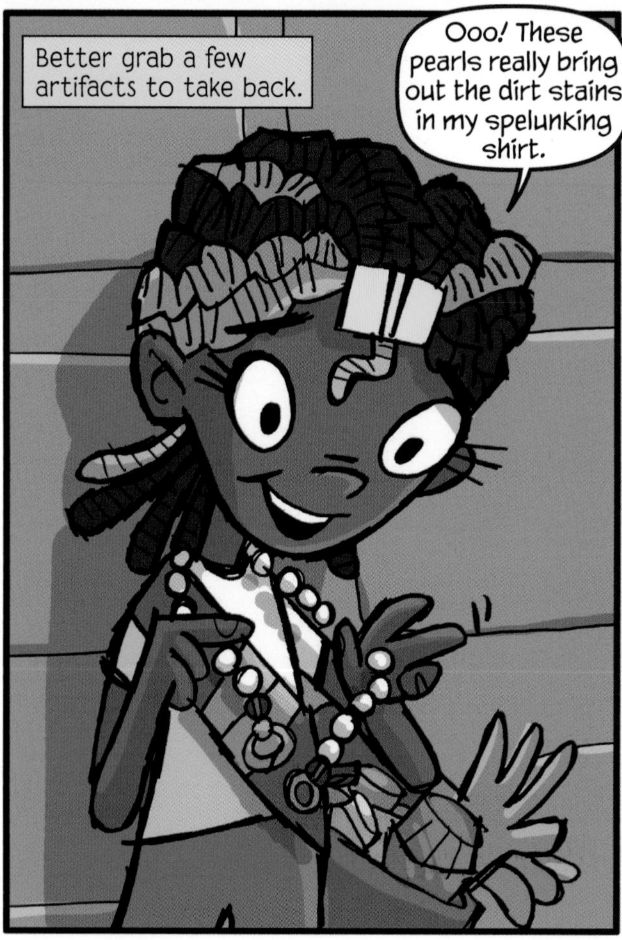
Better grab a few artifacts to take back.
Ooo! These pearls really bring out the dirt stains in my spelunking shirt.

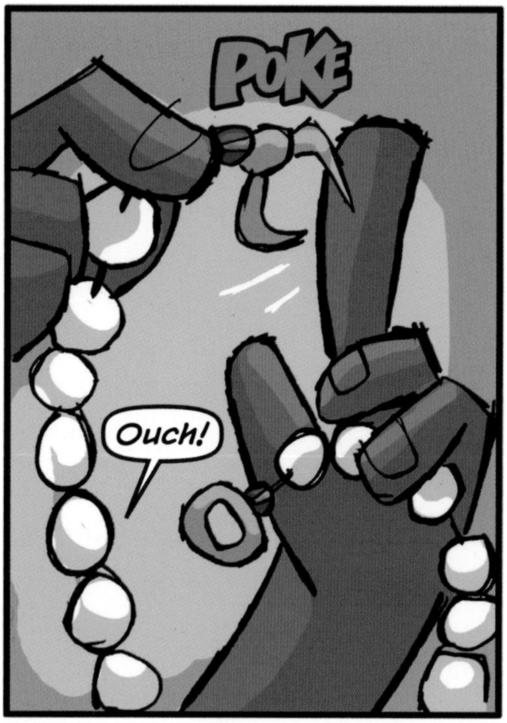
POKE
Ouch!

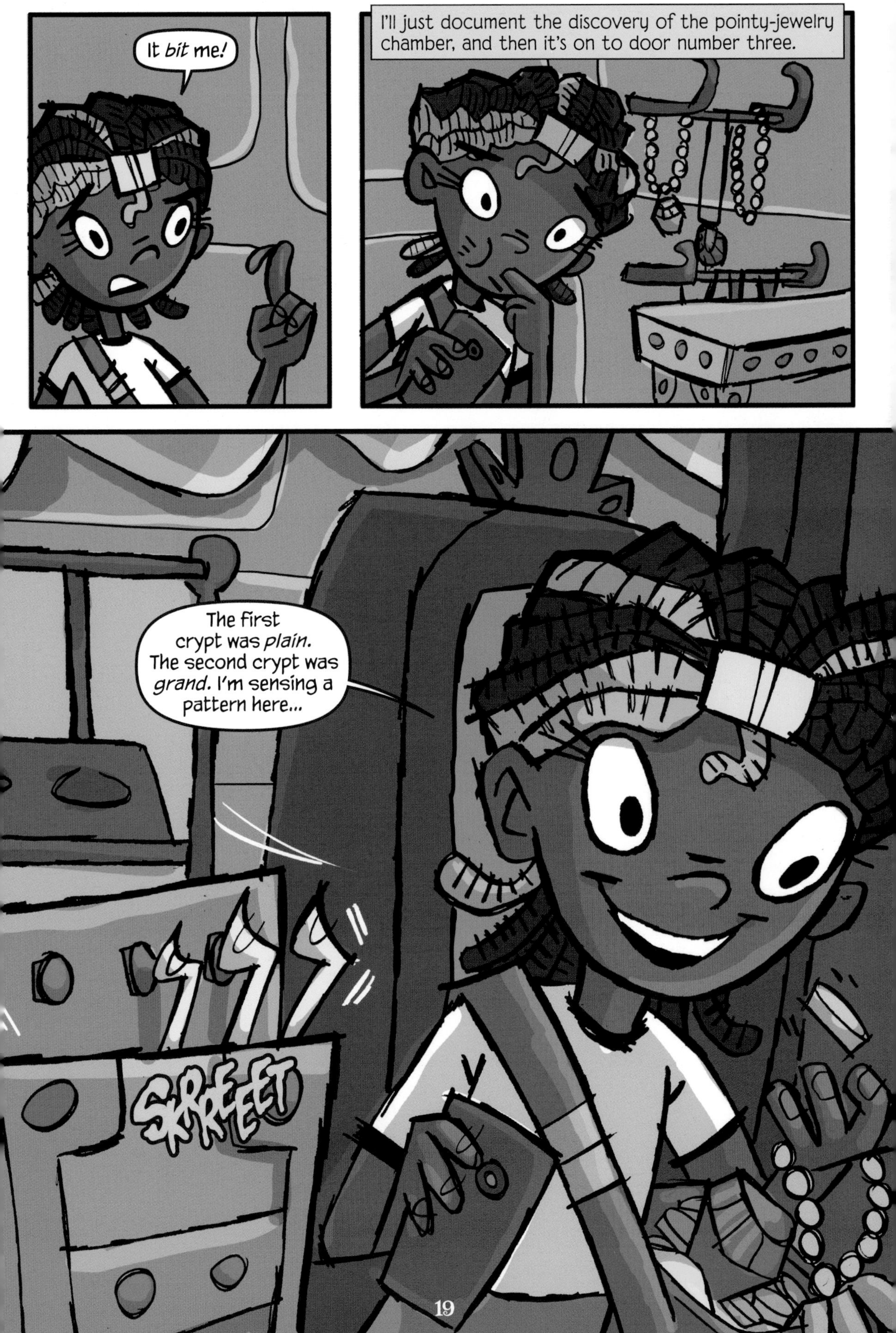
It *bit* me!
I'll just document the discovery of the pointy-jewelry chamber, and then it's on to door number three.
The first crypt was *plain*. The second crypt was *grand*. I'm sensing a pattern here...
SKRREEET

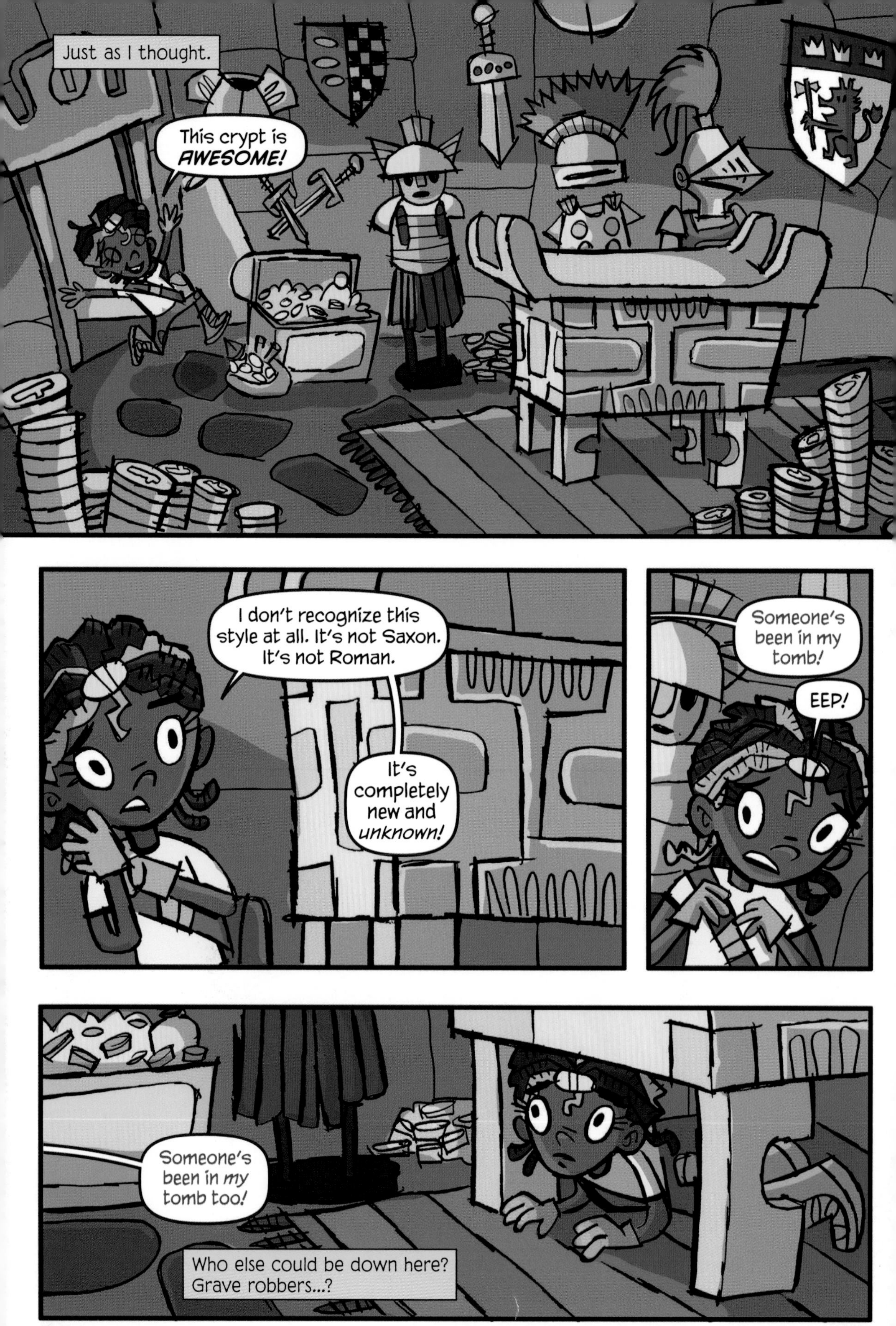

Just as I thought.
This crypt is *AWESOME!*
I don't recognize this style at all. It's not Saxon. It's not Roman.
It's completely new and *unknown!*
Someone's been in my tomb!
EEP!
Someone's been in *my* tomb too!
Who else could be down here? Grave robbers...?

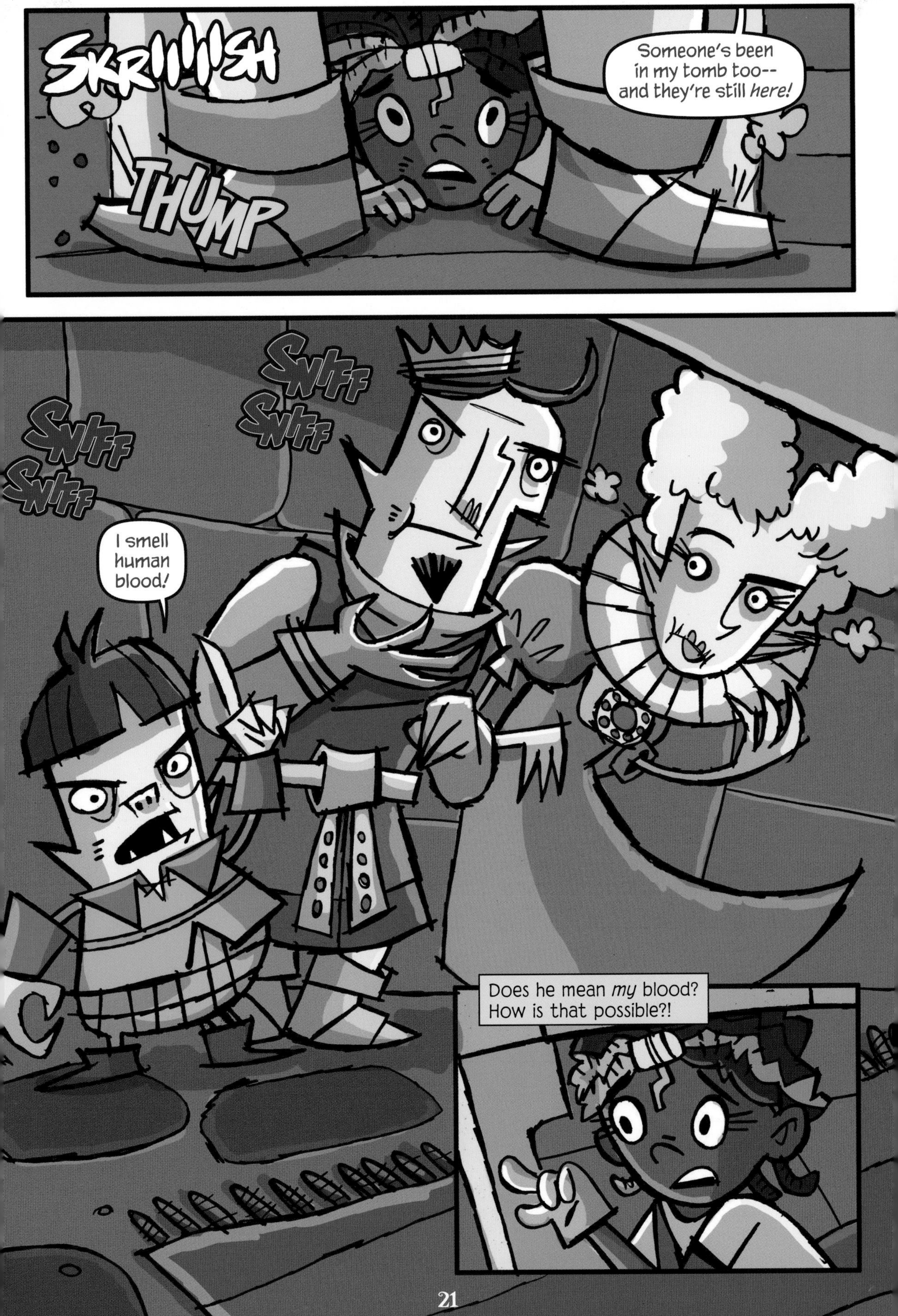
SKRIIIIISH
THUMP
Someone's been in my tomb too--and they're still *here!*
SNIFF SNIFF
SNIFF SNIFF
I smell human blood!
Does he mean *my* blood? How is that possible?!

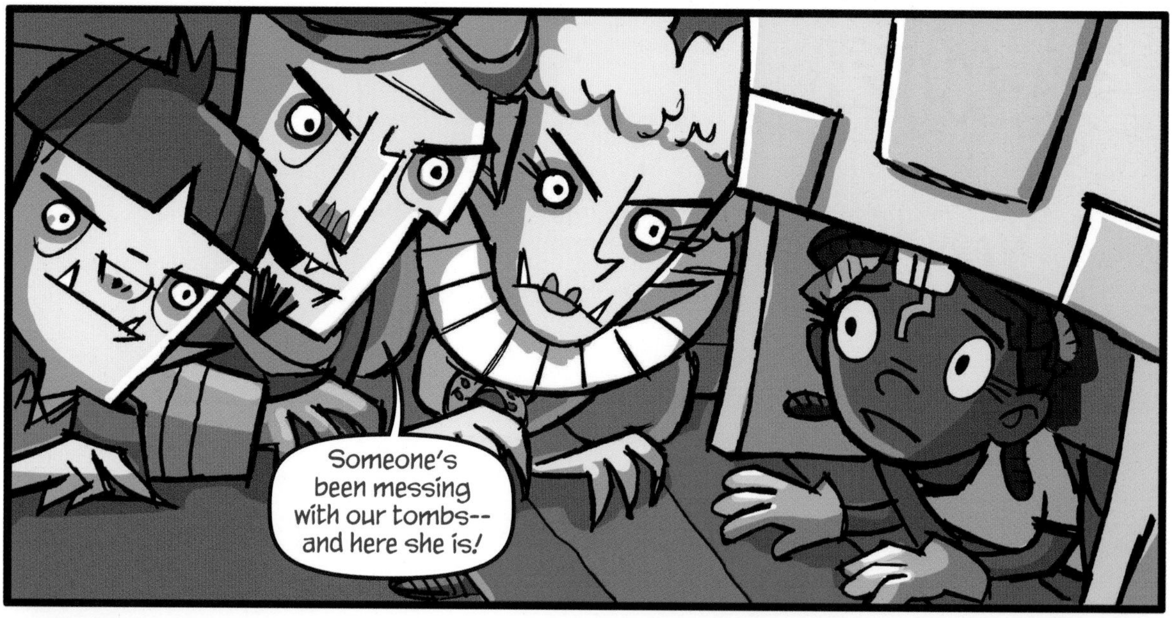
Someone's been messing with our tombs--and here she is!

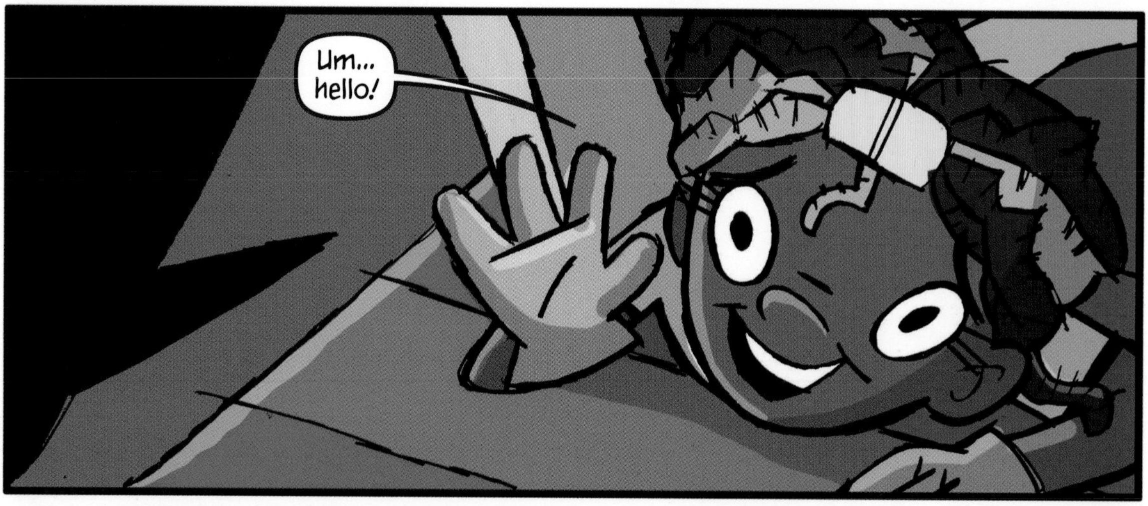
Um... hello!

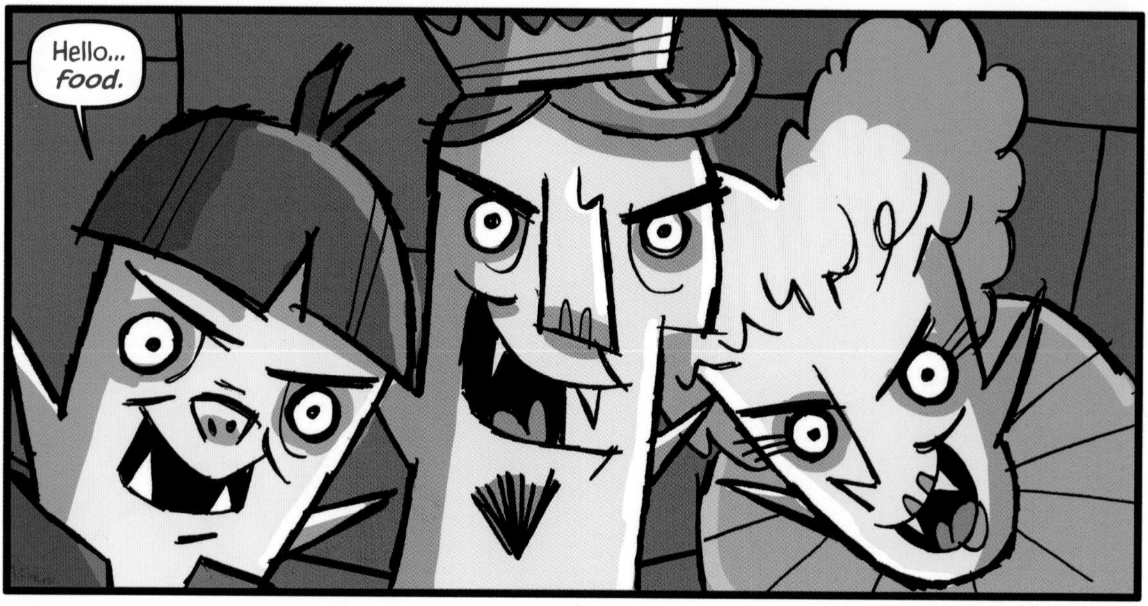
Hello... *food*.

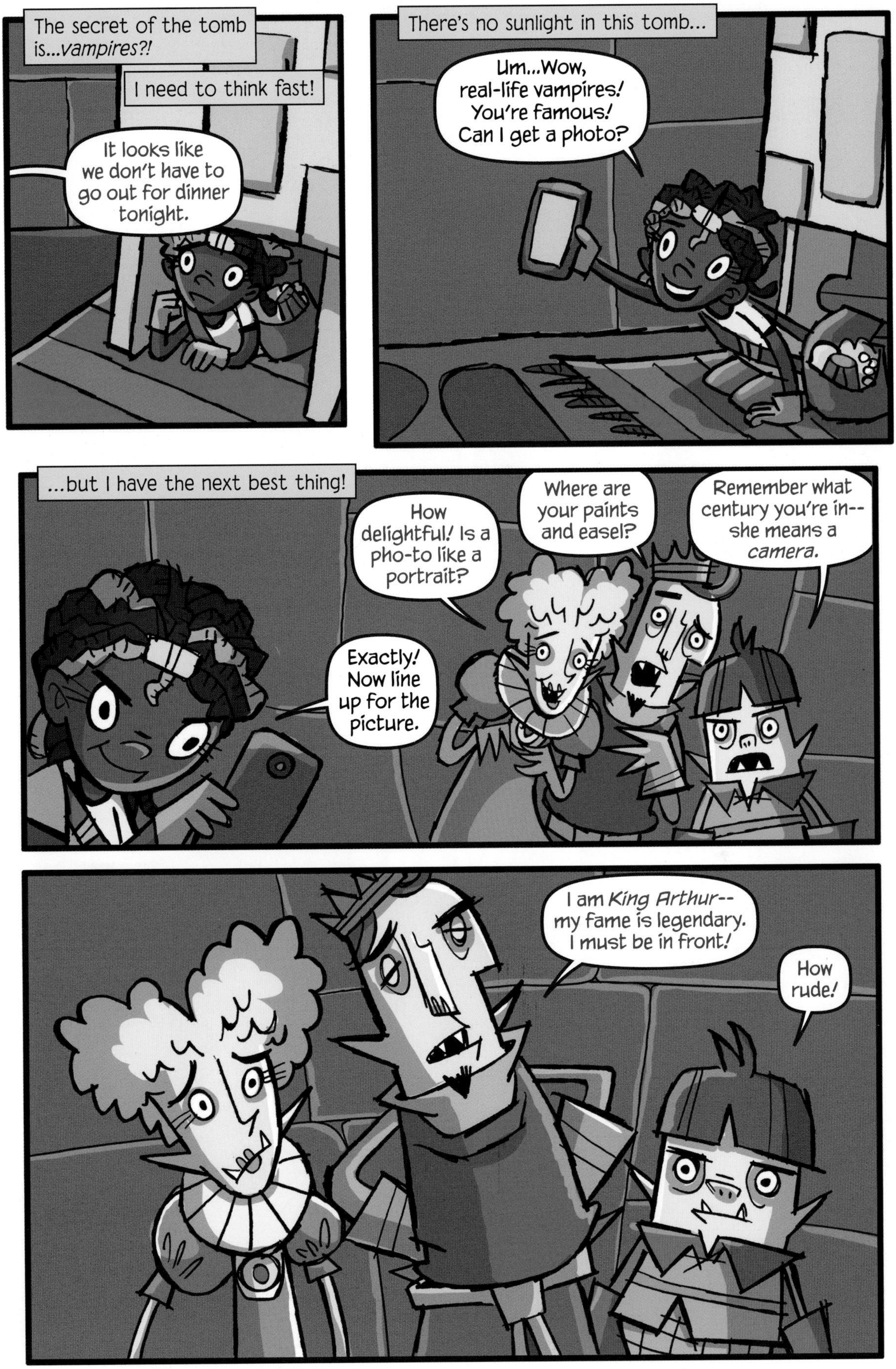
The secret of the tomb is...*vampires?!*
I need to think fast!
It looks like we don't have to go out for dinner tonight.
There's no sunlight in this tomb...
Um...Wow, real-life vampires! You're famous! Can I get a photo?
...but I have the next best thing!
How delightful! Is a pho-to like a portrait?
Where are your paints and easel?
Remember what century you're in--she means a *camera.*
Exactly! Now line up for the picture.
I am *King Arthur*--my fame is legendary. I must be in front!
How rude!

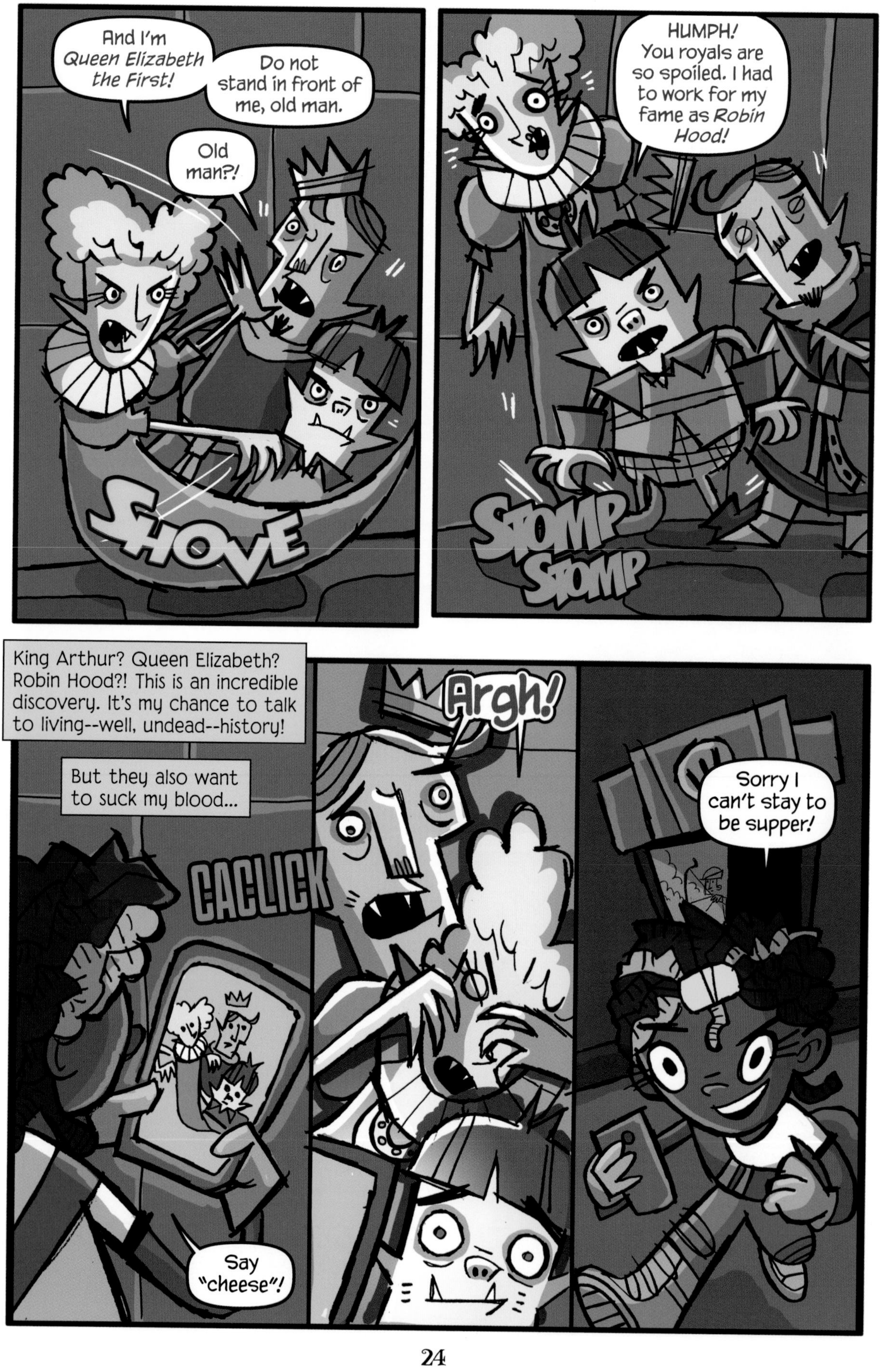
And I'm Queen Elizabeth the First!
Do not stand in front of me, old man.
Old man?!
SHOVE
HUMPH! You royals are so spoiled. I had to work for my fame as Robin Hood!
STOMP
STOMP
King Arthur? Queen Elizabeth? Robin Hood?! This is an incredible discovery. It's my chance to talk to living--well, undead--history!
But they also want to suck my blood...
CACLICK
Say "cheese"!
Argh!
Sorry I can't stay to be supper!

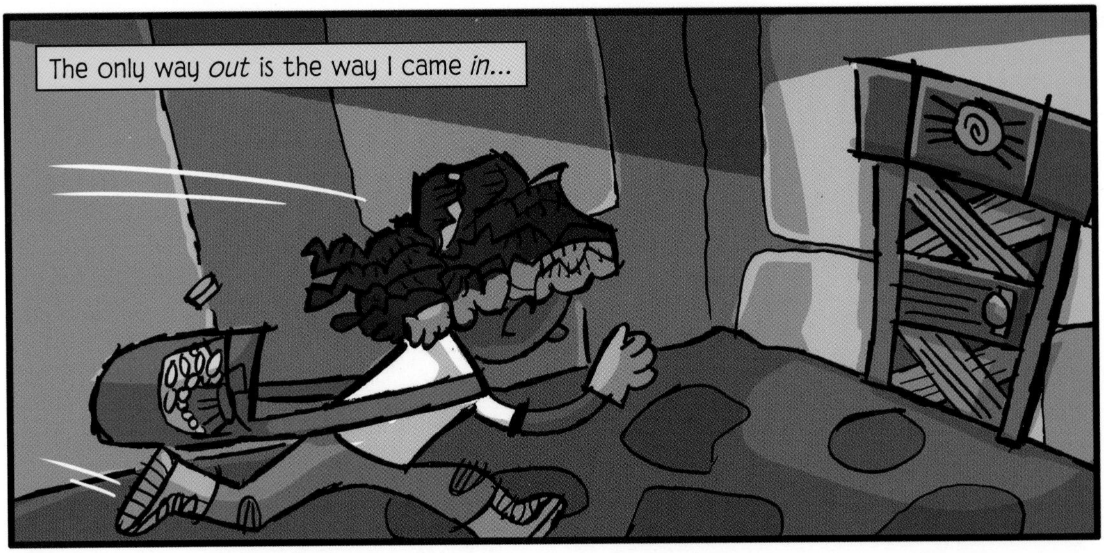
The only way *out* is the way I came *in*...

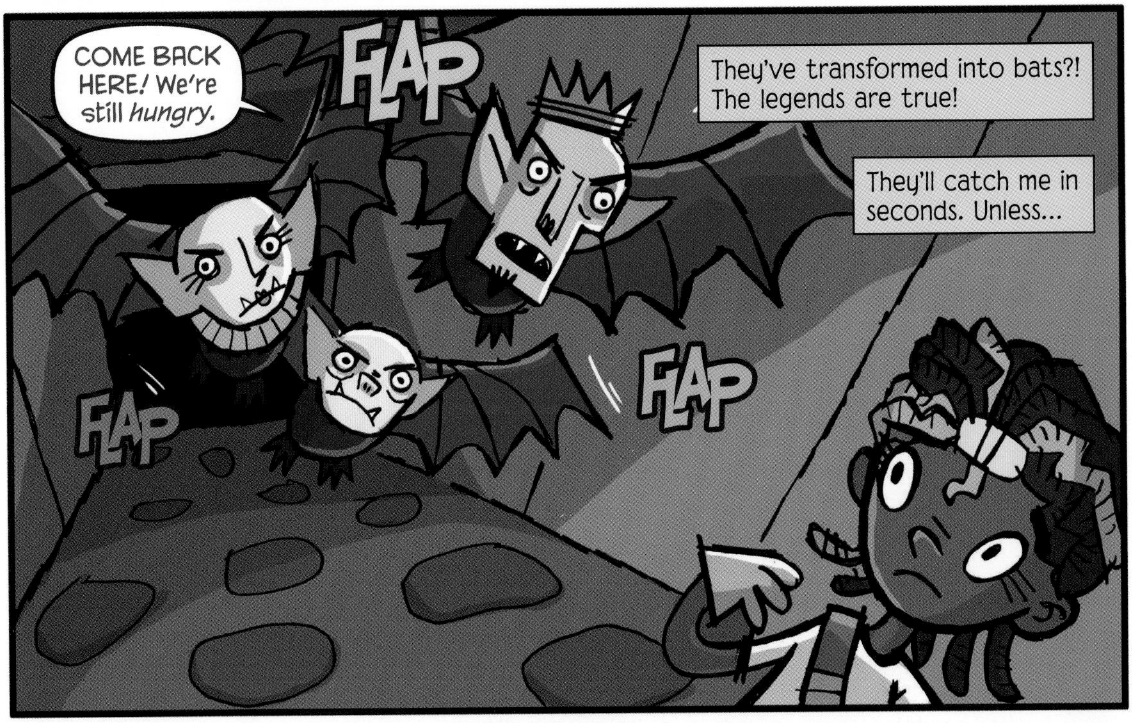
COME BACK HERE! We're still *hungry*.
FLAP
They've transformed into bats?! The legends are true!
They'll catch me in seconds. Unless...
FLAP
FLAP

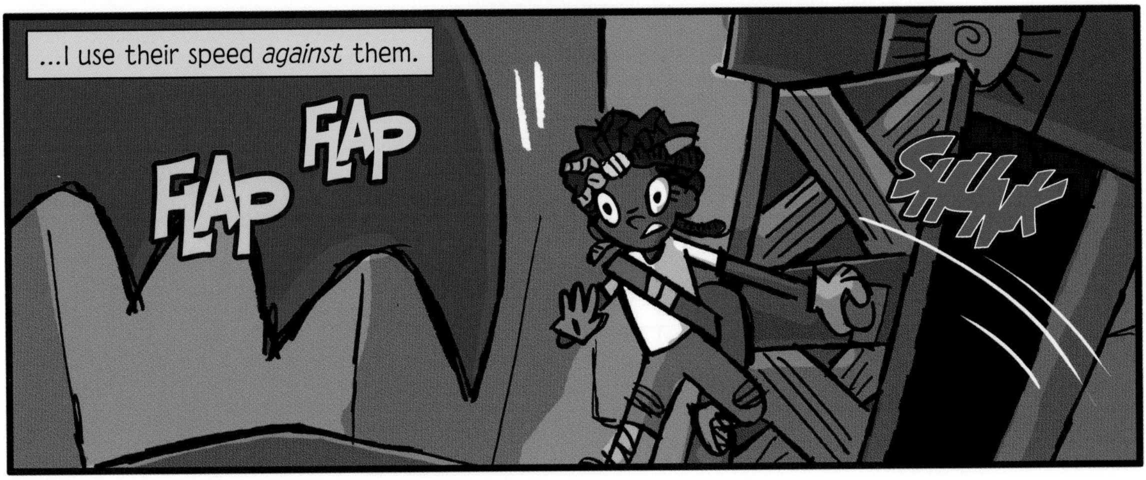
...I use their speed *against* them.
FLAP
FLAP

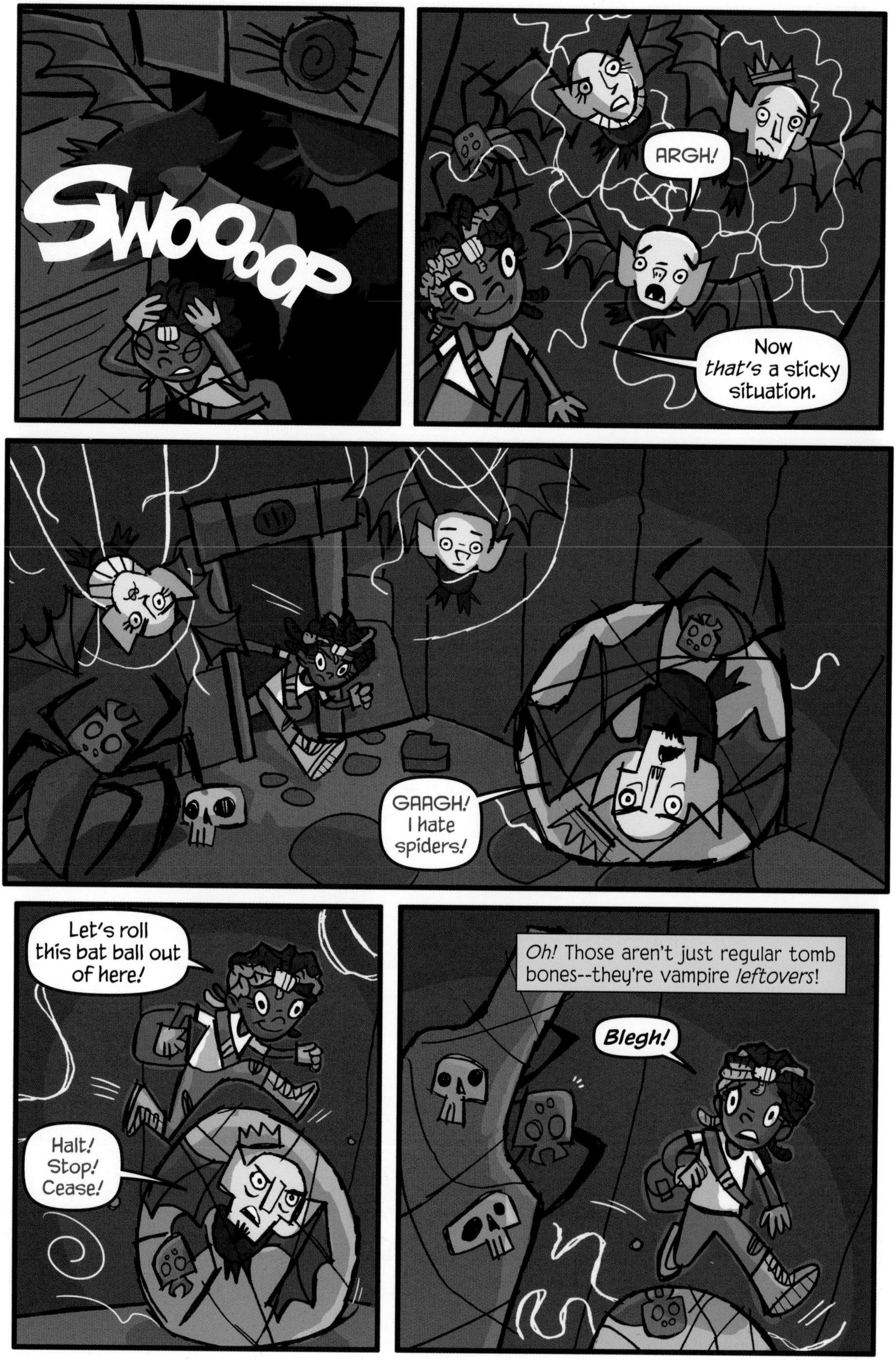
SWOOOOP
ARGH!
Now *that's* a sticky situation.
GAAGH! I hate spiders!
Let's roll this bat ball out of here!
Halt! Stop! Cease!
Oh! Those aren't just regular tomb bones--they're vampire *leftovers*!
Blegh!

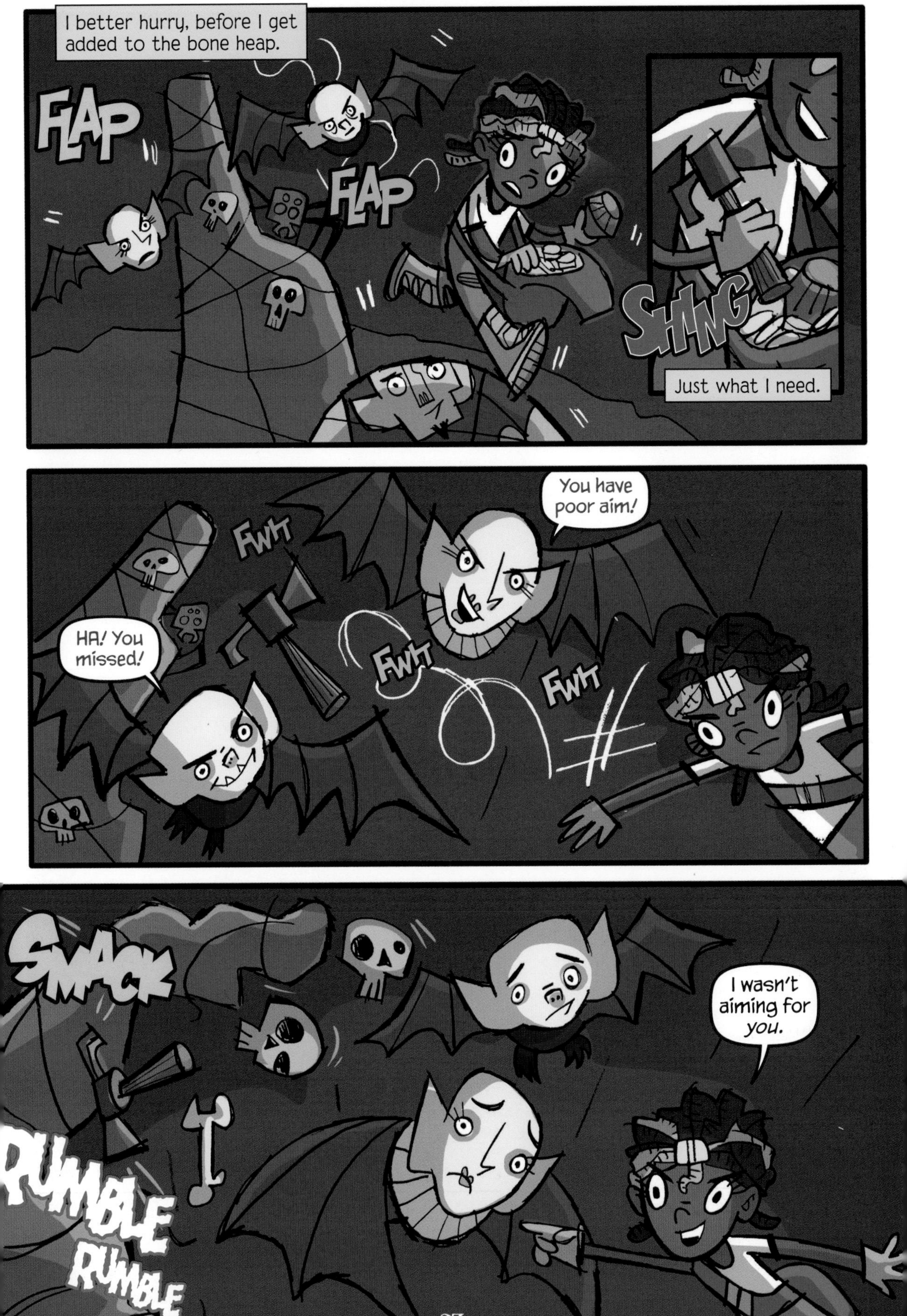

I better hurry, before I get added to the bone heap.
FLAP
FLAP
SHING
Just what I need.
FWIT
You have poor aim!
HA! You missed!
FWIT
FWIT
SMACK
I wasn't aiming for you.
RUMBLE
RUMBLE

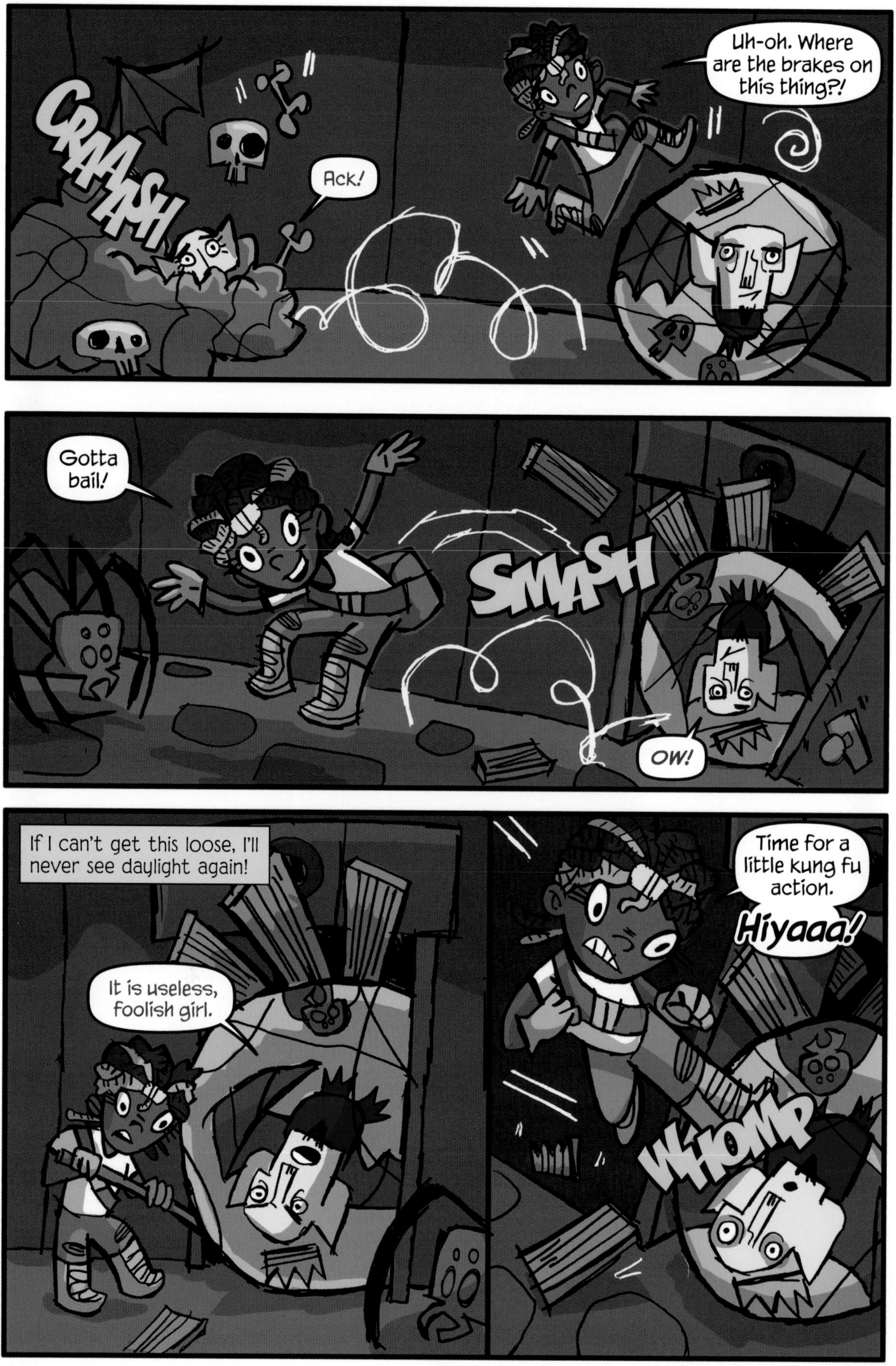
CRAAASH
Ack!
Uh-oh. Where are the brakes on this thing?!
Gotta bail!
SMASH
OW!
If I can't get this loose, I'll never see daylight again!
It is useless, foolish girl.
Time for a little kung fu action.
Hiyaaa!
WHOMP

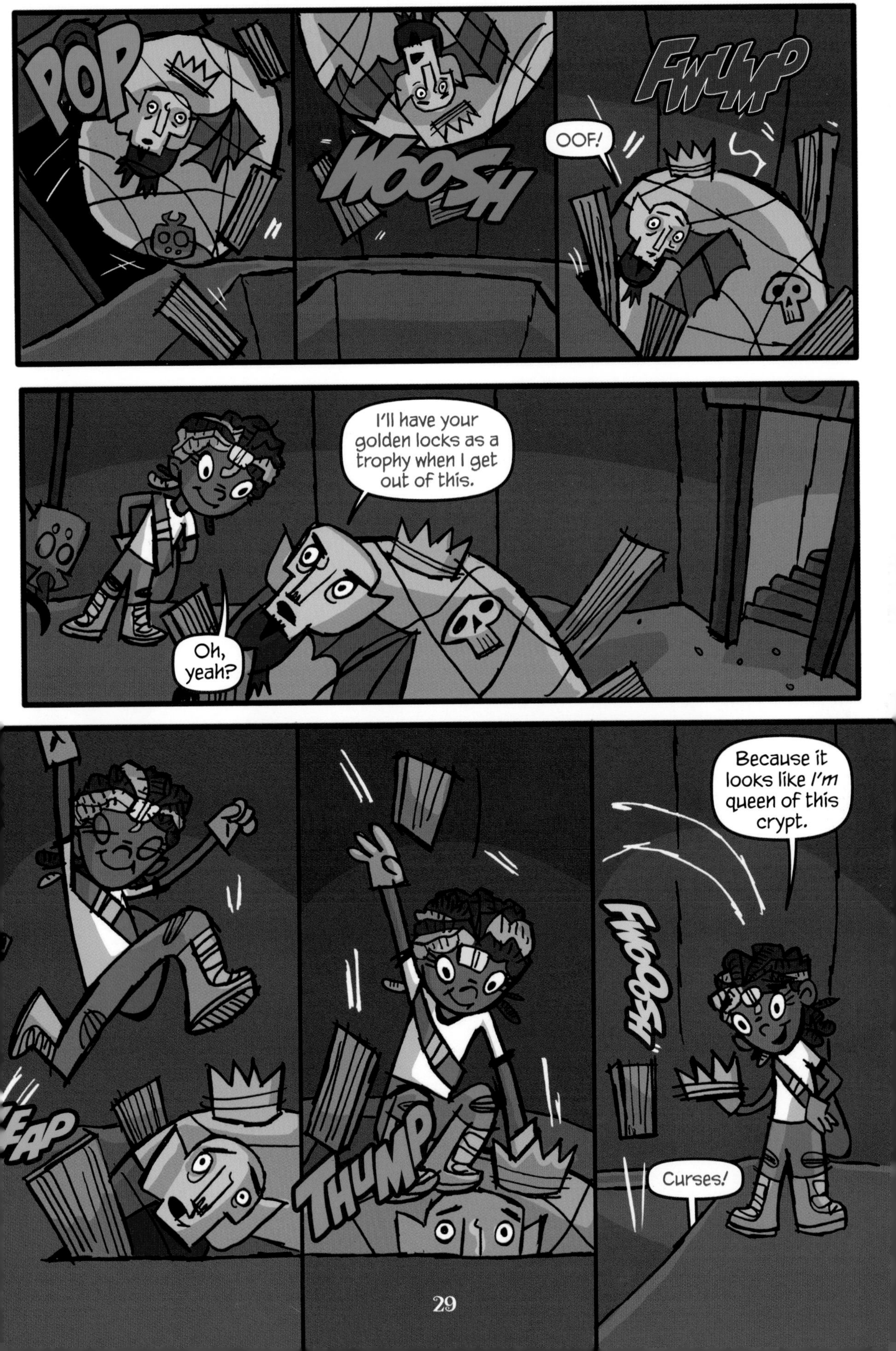
POP
WOOSH
FWUMP
OOF!
I'll have your golden locks as a trophy when I get out of this.
Oh, yeah?
THUMP
Because it looks like *I'm* queen of this crypt.
FWOOSH
Curses!

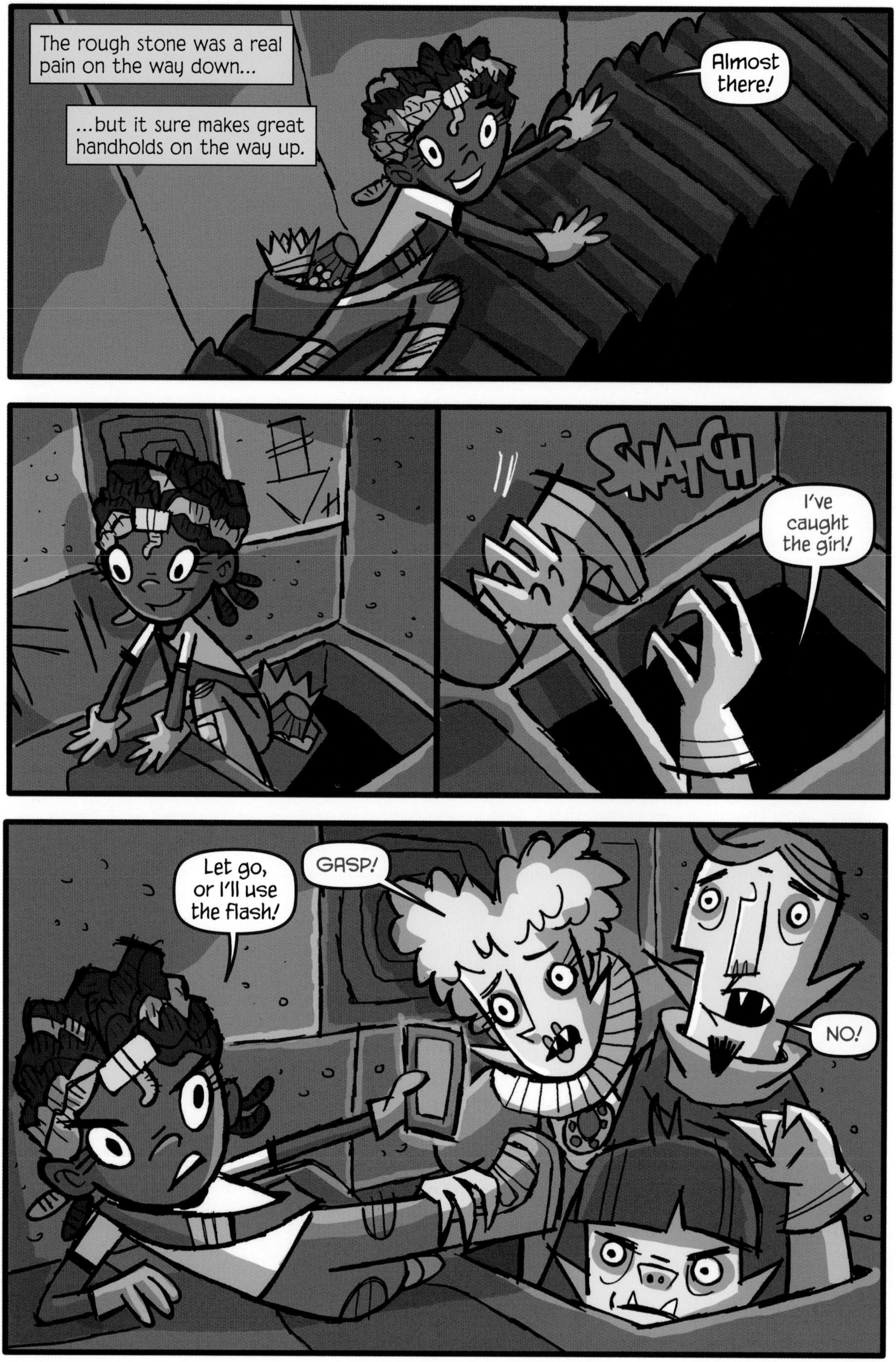
The rough stone was a real pain on the way down...
...but it sure makes great handholds on the way up.
Almost there!
SNATCH
I've caught the girl!
Let go, or I'll use the flash!
GASP!
NO!

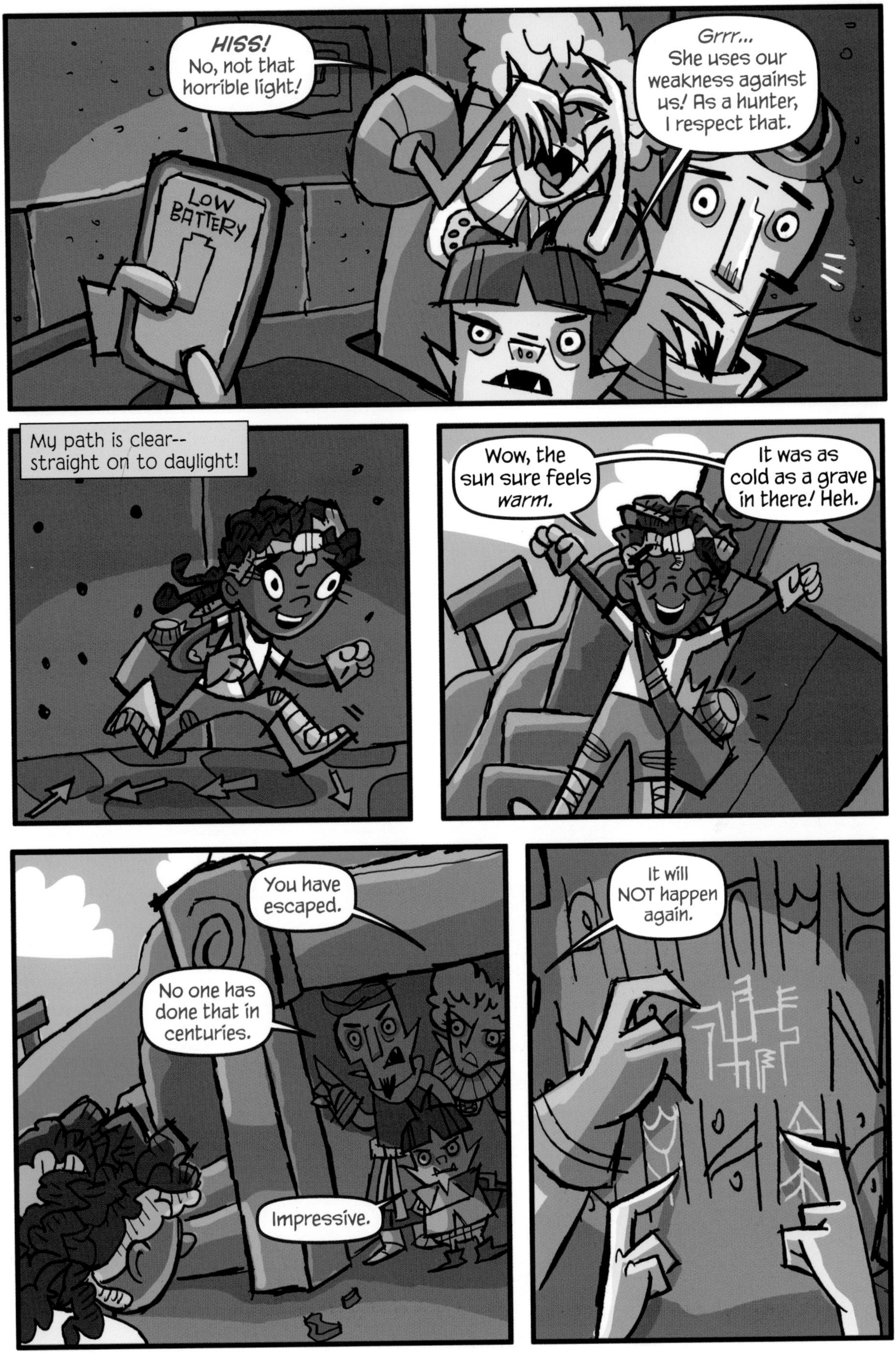
HISS!
No, not that horrible light!
Grrr...
She uses our weakness against us! As a hunter, I respect that.
LOW BATTERY
My path is clear-- straight on to daylight!
Wow, the sun sure feels *warm.*
It was as cold as a grave in there! Heh.
You have escaped.
No one has done that in centuries.
Impressive.
It will NOT happen again.

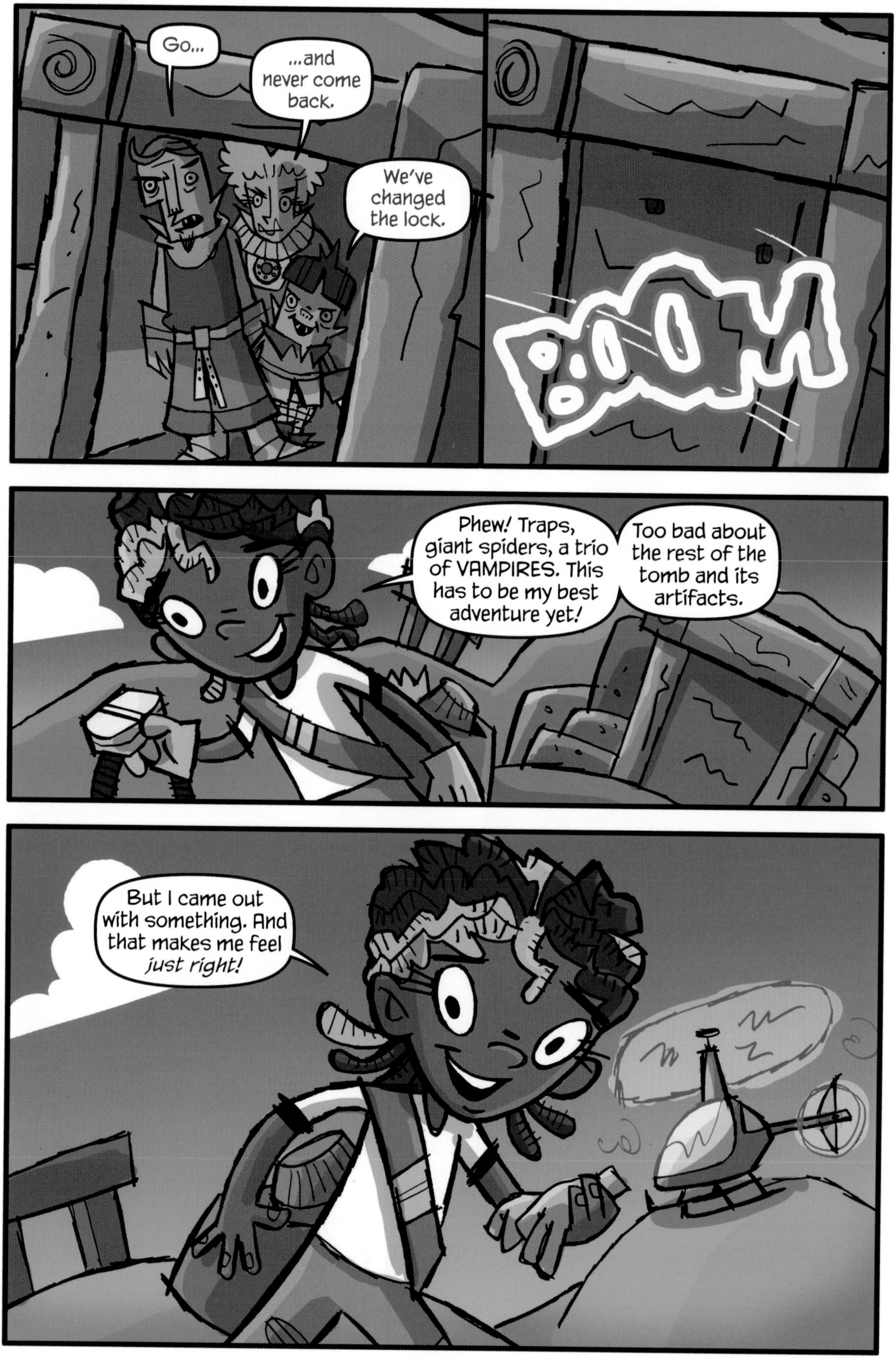
Go...
...and never come back.
We've changed the lock.
BOOM!
Phew! Traps, giant spiders, a trio of VAMPIRES. This has to be my best adventure yet!
Too bad about the rest of the tomb and its artifacts.
But I came out with something. And that makes me feel *just right!*

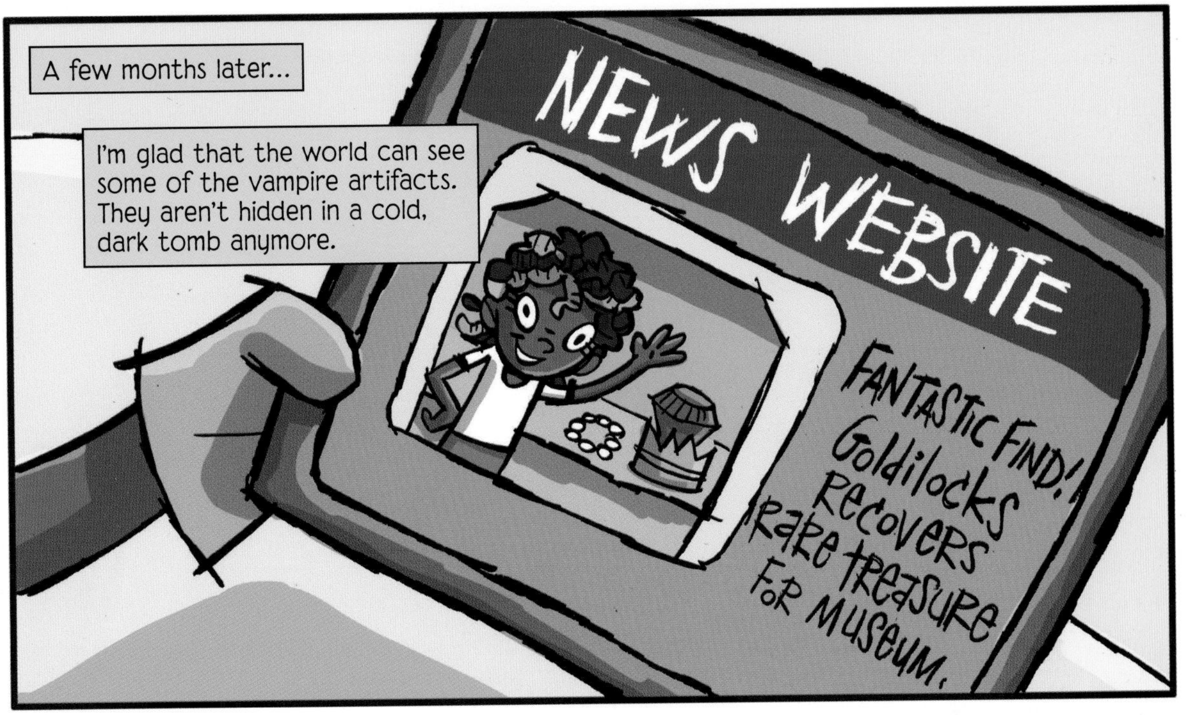
A few months later...
I'm glad that the world can see some of the vampire artifacts. They aren't hidden in a cold, dark tomb anymore.
NEWS WEBSITE
FANTASTIC FIND! Goldilocks Recovers Rare treasure for Museum.

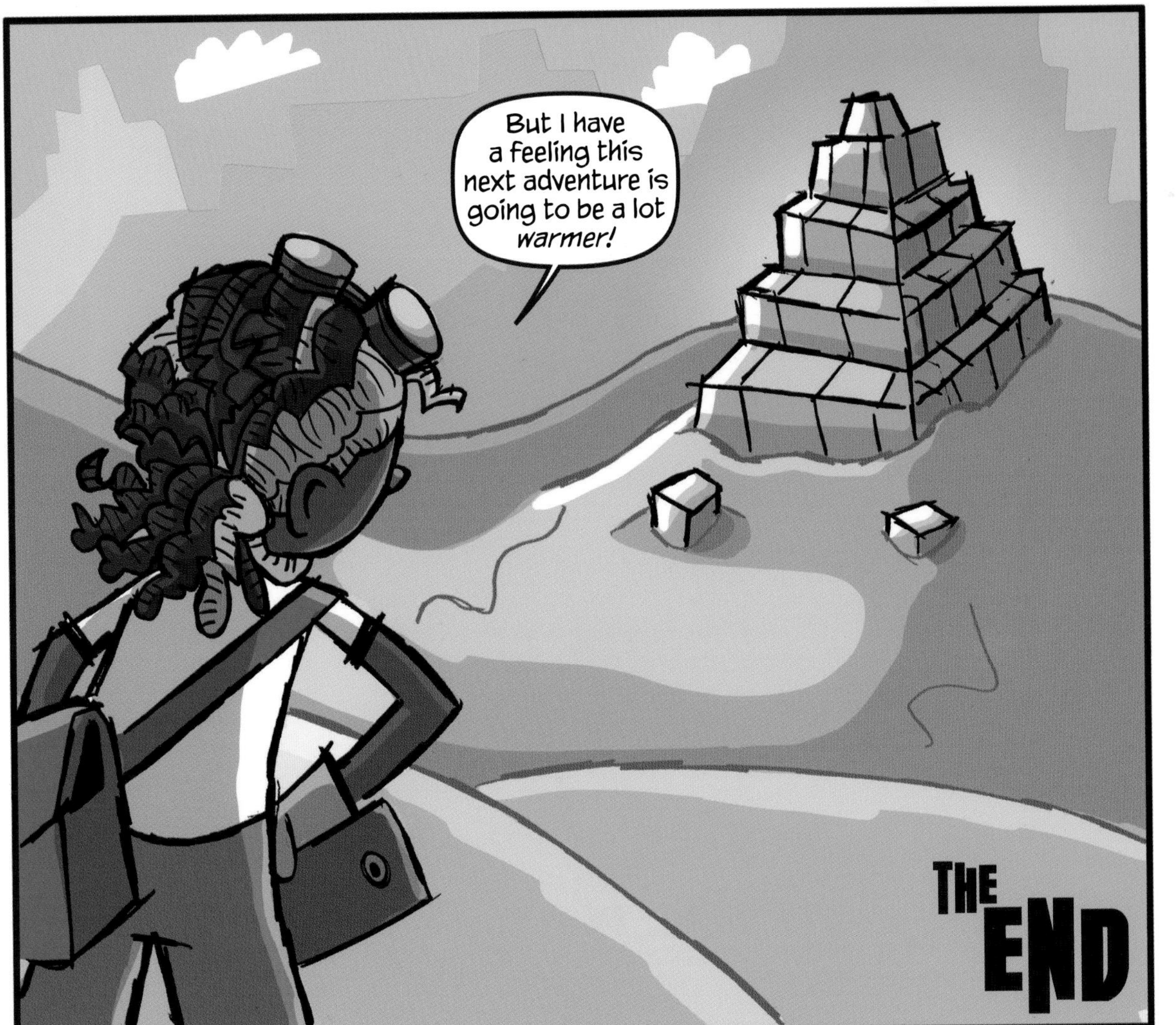
But I have a feeling this next adventure is going to be a lot *warmer!*
THE END

ALL ABOUT THE **ORIGINAL** TALE!

There aren't
any world-famous
crypt crackers in
the original tale, but in
Robert Southey's 1837 version
called "The Story of the Three Bears,"
there is a nosy home intruder!

A little bear, a middle-sized bear, and a big bear live in a house in the woods. One morning, the bears make porridge for breakfast. They decide to go on a walk to give the food time to cool.

Not long after, an old woman comes to the house. She walks right in and sees three bowls of porridge on a table. She tries the porridge from the big bowl--it's too hot. Next she eats from the medium bowl--it's too cold. Finally she eats from the little bowl-- it's neither too hot nor too cold, but just right. So she gobbles it up!

The woman tries out the bears' chairs. Only Little Bear's chair is just right, and she sits in it until it breaks. Then the woman lies in the bears' beds. Once again, only Little Bear's is just right. She falls right to sleep.

The three bears come back for breakfast...only to discover someone's been eating their porridge! They also notice someone's been sitting in their chairs and sleeping in their beds. Little Bear looks at his bed and says, "Someone's been sleeping in my bed--and here she is!"

Little Bear's voice wakes the old woman. She hops out of bed and jumps out an open window never to be seen again.

Later versions of the tale switch out the old woman for a young girl who's playing in the woods. She finds the empty house and decides to explore. The little girl was called Silverhair and Goldenlocks before she was finally called Goldilocks in 1904.

A FAR OUT GUIDE TO HE TALE'S ARCHAEOLOGICAL TWISTS

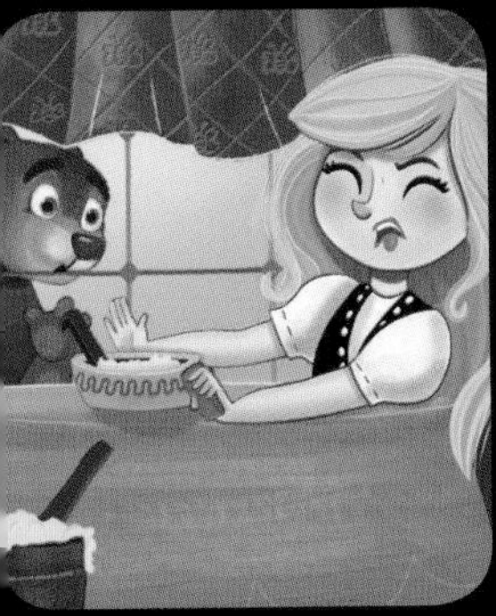

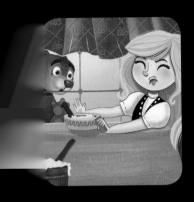

In the original tale, Goldilocks just wanders into someone's house (how rude!). In this version, she's there to study the tomb and its artifacts.

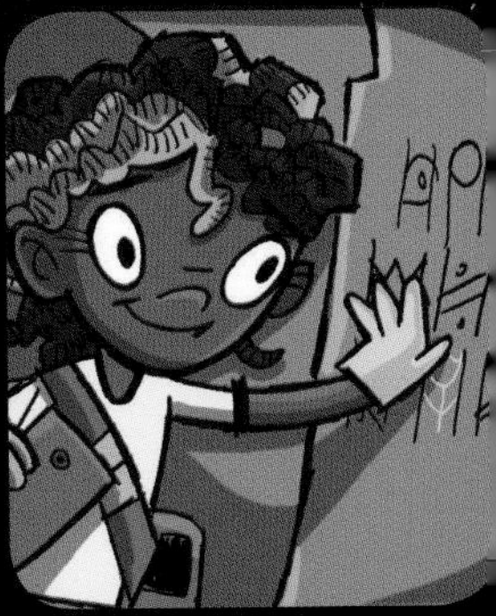

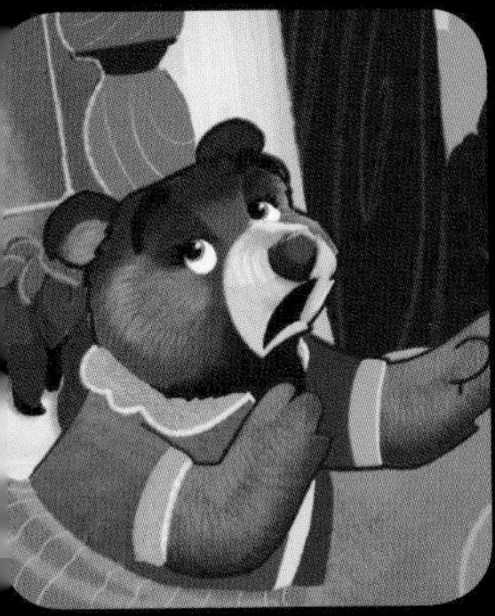

Three bears have been replaced with three blood-sucking vampires!

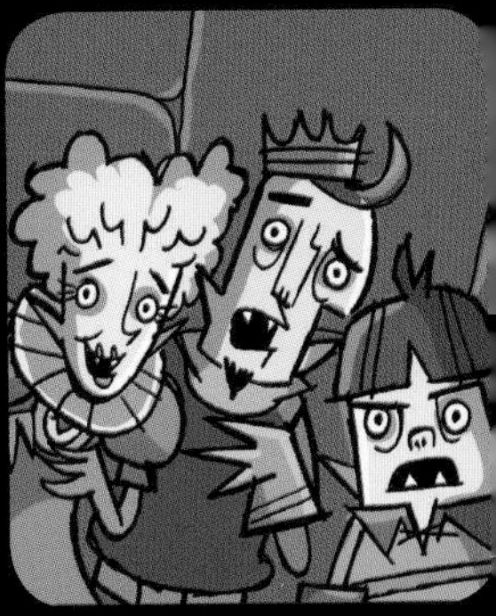

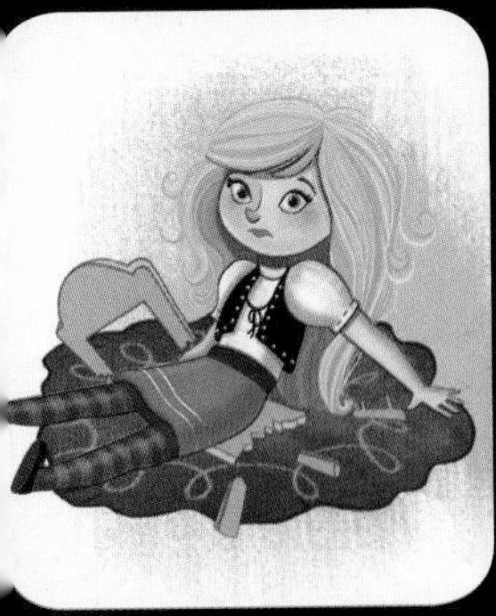

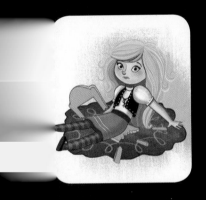

Instead of eating porridge or trying out chairs and beds, Goldi uses her skills to avoid three tricky traps!

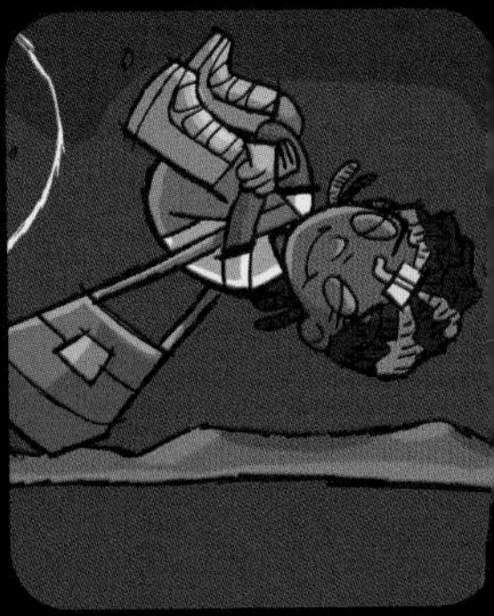

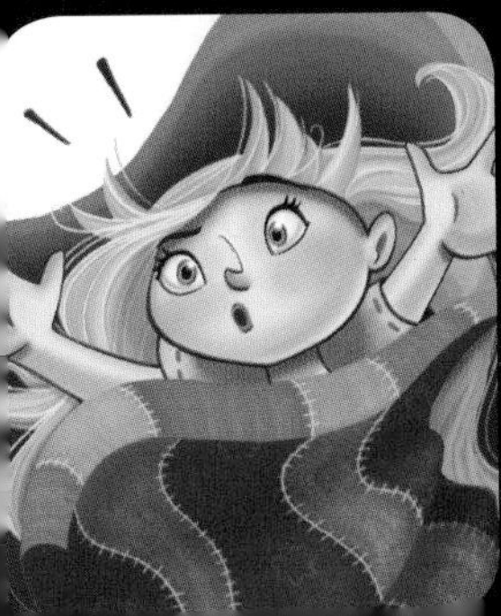

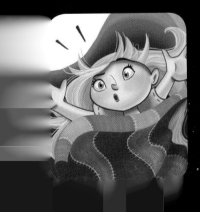

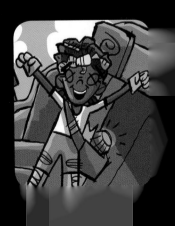

The original Goldilocks is woken up from a nap and runs away. In this tale, she uses her smarts to escape and is ready for more adventure!

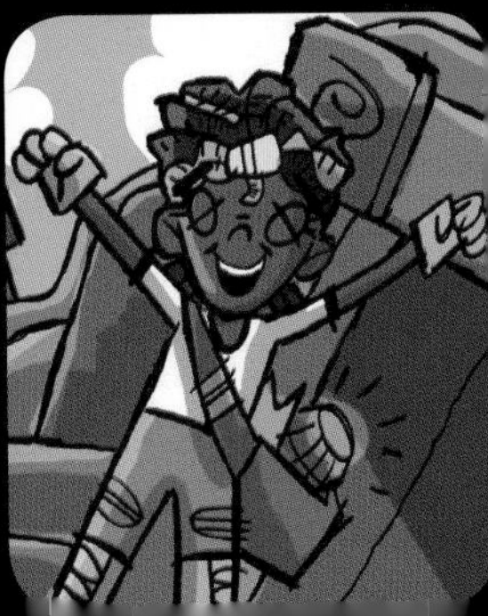

VISUAL QUESTIONS

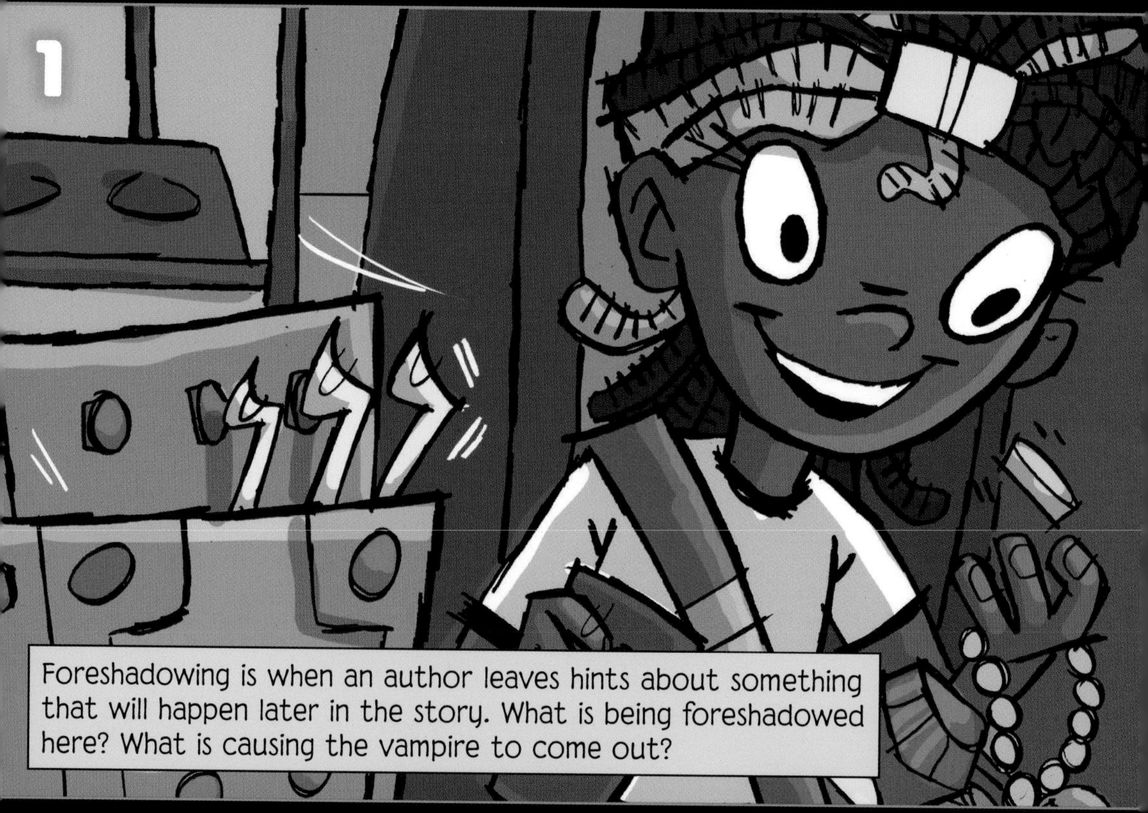
1

Foreshadowing is when an author leaves hints about something that will happen later in the story. What is being foreshadowed here? What is causing the vampire to come out?

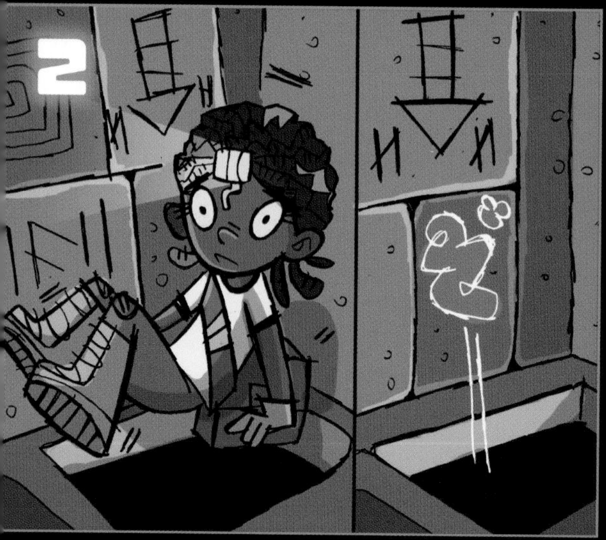
2

In your own words, describe what's happening in these two panels. Look at page 10 if you need help.

What is Goldi about to do at the end of the story? What kind of new creatures might she run into on her next adventure?

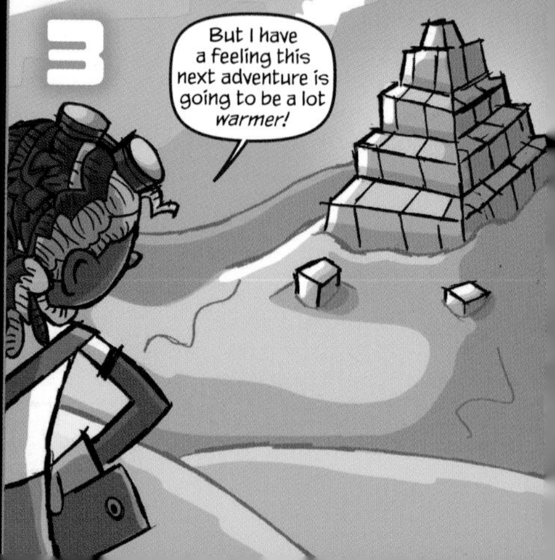
3
But I have a feeling this next adventure is going to be a lot *warmer!*

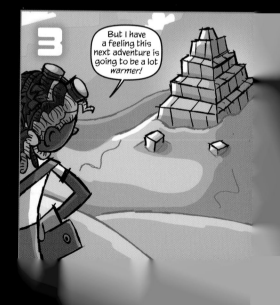

Goldi threatens to use the flash on her phone and is able to escape. But what does the reader know that the vampires don't?

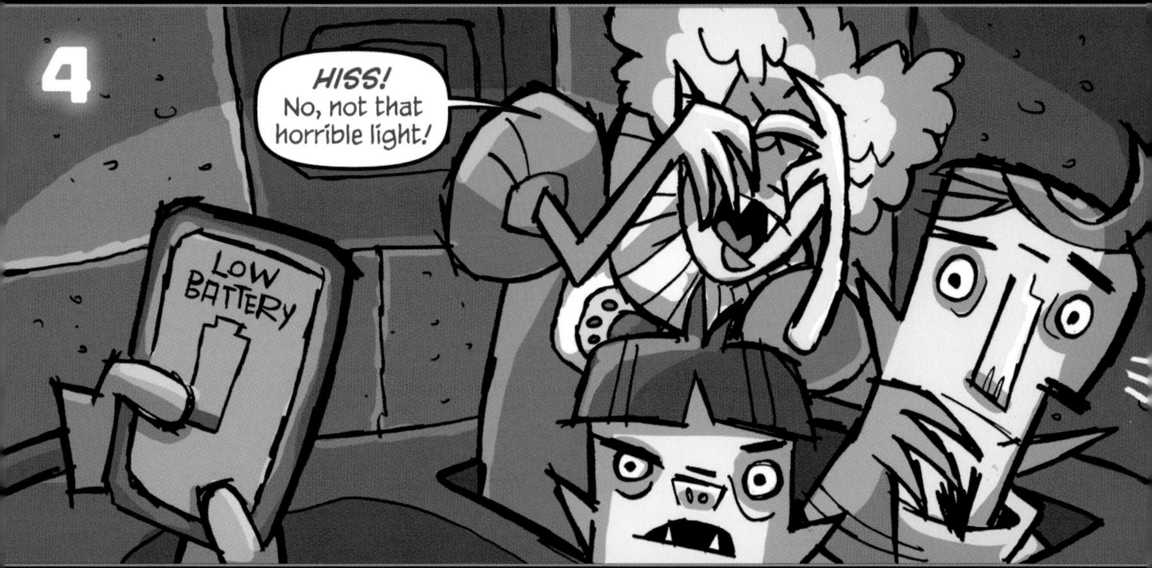
4
HISS!
No, not that horrible light!
LOW BATTERY

Do you think the vampires are really who they say they are? Why or why not? Write a paragraph about your answer.

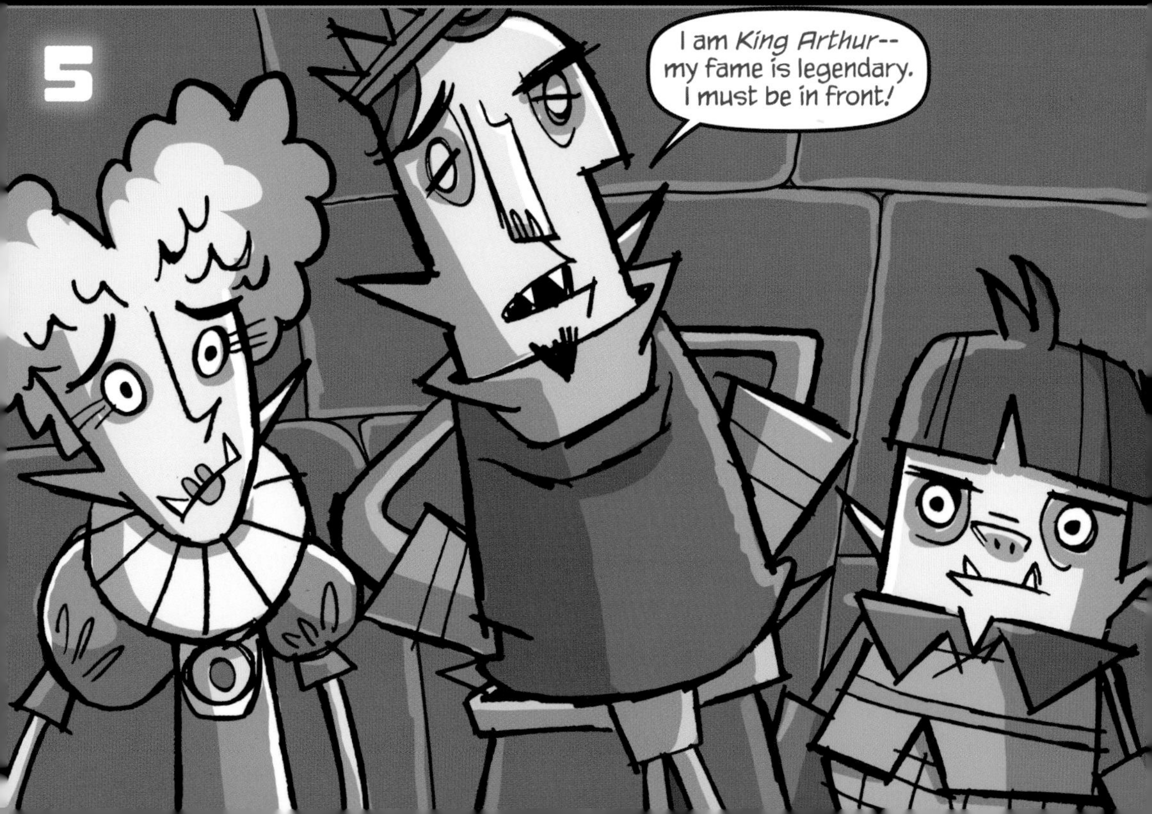
5
I am *King Arthur*-- my fame is legendary. I must be in front!

AUTHOR

Laurie S. Sutton has been reading comics since she was a kid. She grew up to become an editor for Marvel, DC Comics, Starblaze, and Tekno Comics. She has written *Adam Strange* for DC, *Star Trek: Voyager* for Marvel, plus *Star Trek: Deep Space Nine* and *Witch Hunter* for Malibu Comics. There are long boxes of comics in her closet where there should be clothing and shoes. Laurie has lived all over the world but currently resides in Florida.

ILLUSTRATOR

C.S. Jennings loves to draw. He takes his sketchbook and drawing tools wherever he goes. As a freelance illustrator, he draws lots of stuff; like for video games, board games, and books (like this one!).

GLOSSARY

artifacts (AR-tuh-faktss)--objects made and used by humans long ago

constellation (KAHN-stuh-lay-shuhn)--a group of stars that forms a shape, such as an object, animal, or person

crypt (KRIPT)--an underground room, often used as a burial place for the dead (or undead)

document (DAHK-yuh-mehnt)--make note of something through writing, photography, or film to prove that it happened or existed

extraordinaire (ek-stror-duh-NER)--extremely skilled at something

megalithic (MEG-uh-lith-ik)--a megalith is a very large stone used by ancient cultures as part of a building or as a monument. If something is megalithic, it is similar in looks to a megalith.

portrait (POR-trit)--a picture of a person's face and shoulders, often painted or drawn

raiders (REY-derz)--people who enter a place to steal. A tomb raider breaks into tombs in order to steal valuables buried with the dead.

spelunking (spi-LUHNGK-ing)--the activity of exploring caves. A spelunking shirt is a shirt designed specially for the exploration of caves.

tomb (TOOM)--a grave, room, or building for holding dead bodies

transform (trans-FORM)--change a great deal, such as in your actions or appearance

vibrations (vye-BRAY-shuhnz)--fast movement back and forth

AWESOMELY EVER AFTER.

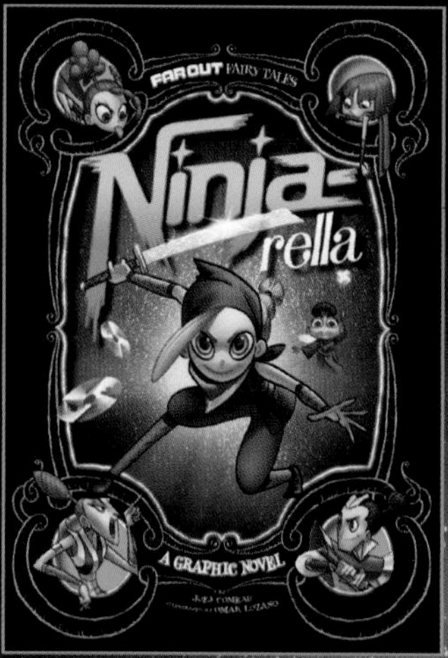
FAR OUT FAIRY TALES
Ninja-rella
A GRAPHIC NOVEL

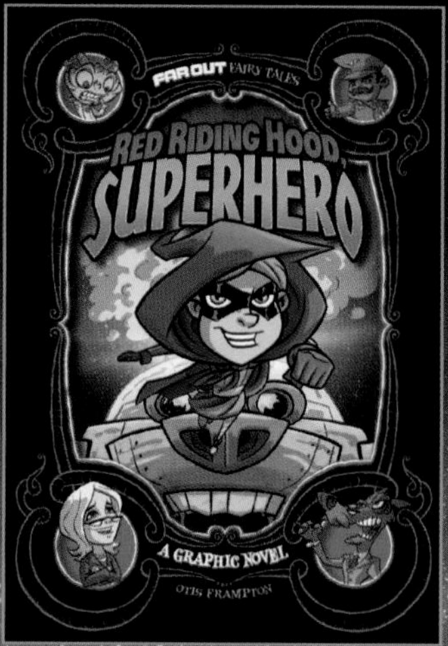
FAR OUT FAIRY TALES
RED RIDING HOOD SUPERHERO
A GRAPHIC NOVEL
OTIS FRAMPTON

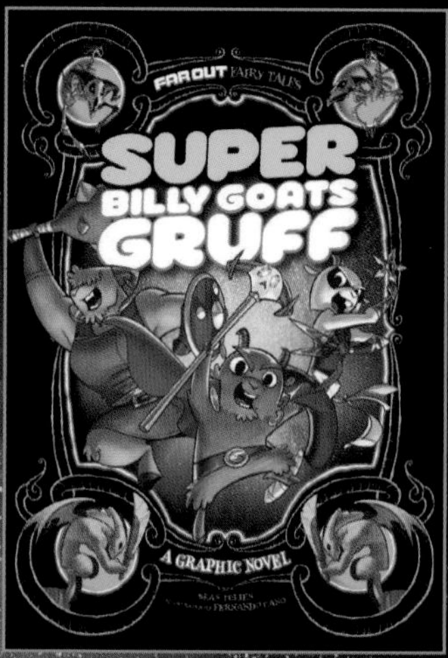
FAR OUT FAIRY TALES
SUPER BILLY GOATS GRUFF
A GRAPHIC NOVEL

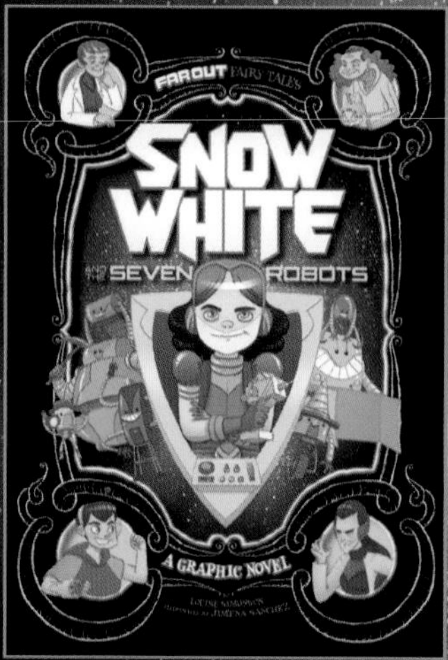
FAR OUT FAIRY TALES
SNOW WHITE AND THE SEVEN ROBOTS
A GRAPHIC NOVEL

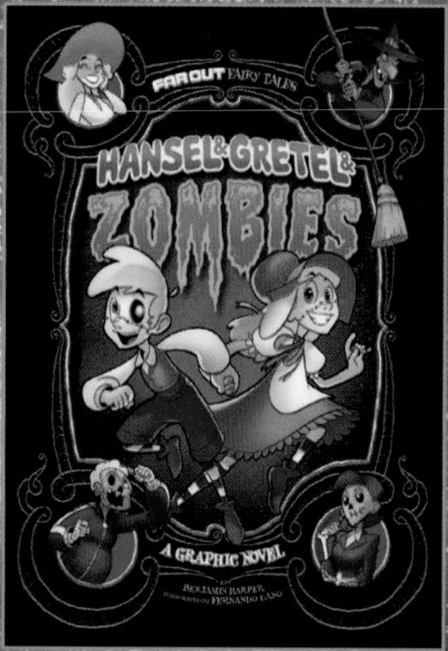
FAR OUT FAIRY TALES
HANSEL & GRETEL & ZOMBIES
A GRAPHIC NOVEL

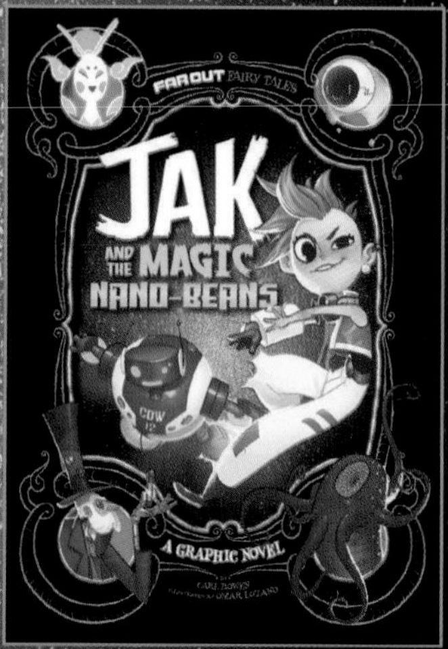
FAR OUT FAIRY TALES
JAK AND THE MAGIC NANO-BEANS
A GRAPHIC NOVEL

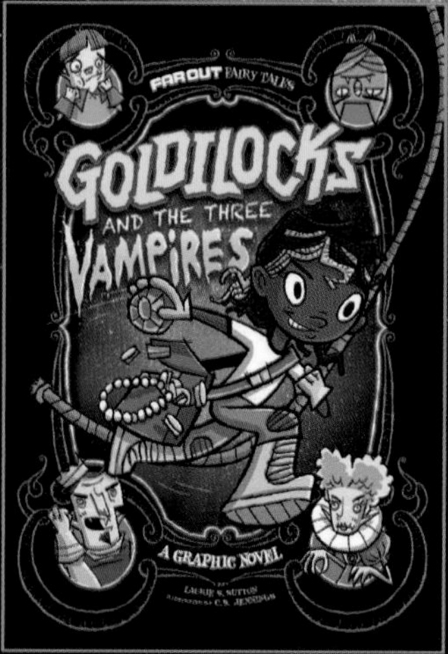
FAR OUT FAIRY TALES
GOLDILOCKS AND THE THREE VAMPIRES
A GRAPHIC NOVEL

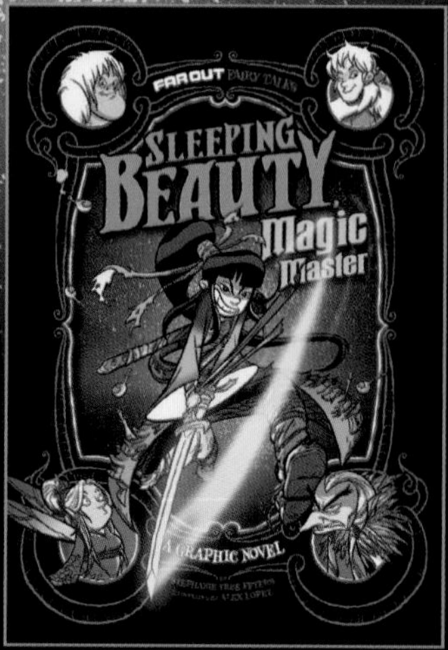
FAR OUT FAIRY TALES
SLEEPING BEAUTY Magic Master
A GRAPHIC NOVEL

FAR OUT FAIRY TALES